A PASSING GRADE FOR THE COWBOY

ELK MOUNTAIN RANCH BOOK THREE

RUTH PENDLETON

CONTENTS

Wedding bells were in the air, and no matter which way Reid Matthews turned, he couldn't escape them. He walked into the kitchen for a drink after plowing one of the fields to find his brother, Porter, flipping through a bridal magazine. It wasn't typical reading material for the rugged cowboy, but Porter seemed just as excited as his fiancé about making plans.

"Nice reading," Reid said. He pushed aside a stack of fabric that was precariously perched on the counter, huffing as he did so. The kitchen was supposed to be a wedding-free zone, but it was beginning to look like a craft store had thrown up all over every available space. No one else in the family was bothered by the mess. In fact, the entire family had been bitten by the wedding bug.

Porter looked up from the magazine, his deep brown eyes crinkling with laughter. "What's wrong, Reid? You're telling me you haven't wanted to pick up one of the five hundred bridal magazines laying around the house?"

Reid shook his head. "The women don't even live here. Can't the planning happen at Emily's house? Or Hazel's?"

Right on cue, the women entered the kitchen, animatedly talking. Emily headed straight for Porter's open arms.

"You're doing your homework!" she exclaimed. She kissed Porter's cheek and looked at her soon to be brother-in-law. "Reid, have you picked out your suit for the wedding yet?"

Thomas leaned back against the counter, folding his arms. "Yeah, Reid. Have you picked out your suit?"

Reid took a drink of water and pretended to swallow the wrong way. He shook his head as he left the room coughing. That would buy him a little more time before he had to answer. Choosing a suit should be an easy task, but Reid couldn't force himself to get to a fitting. He was resentful of his brothers and the fact that they were asking him to focus on yet another task when he was already drowning in his own responsibilities.

The fact that both of his older brothers were planning weddings put a lot of pressure on Reid's shoulders. He was no longer able to hide behind his brothers when it came to dating. Now all eyes were turning to him. The gossip was already starting.

Mrs. Landon lived right down the road, close enough for her eagle eyes to catch everything going on at the Matthews family ranch. With Porter and Reid both proposing on her tulip fields, she felt the need to insert herself into the family's business whenever she could. She had started the gossip, loudly asking Reid after their

Sunday meeting if he was looking to join his brothers in wedded bliss.

"My niece Sherry is coming for a visit this summer," she said, pulling out her phone. "That's when Porter's getting married, right?" She shoved a picture of Sherry in Reid's face. The woman in the picture wasn't bad looking, but Reid wasn't interested in dating someone old enough to be his mom.

Reid squeezed the brim of his hat, working to keep his voice light. "Thomas and Hazel are the ones getting married in the summer. Porter and Emily are in the fall."

"That's right. Sherry will be here to visit next week. I'll introduce you." She spun to walk away briskly, taking with her the retort on Reid's lips.

"That's just great," Reid muttered. He was almost to his car when Gideon, the town baker, called his name.

"Hold up a minute, Reid," Gideon yelled. He jogged to Reid's side, his face flushed by the time he reached him. "I've been trying to get ahold of your brother Porter, but I keep getting an error message. I must have written his number down wrong."

Reid pulled out his phone to double check the number. Gideon had mixed up the last two digits.

"Thanks. I figured that it was something like that."

"Any time," Reid said. He tried to walk back to his car, but Gideon fell in step beside him.

"I'm making the cake for Porter and Emily, and puff pastries for Thomas and Hazel. Rumor has it that you are also planning your wedding. Who's the lucky lady?"

Mortification flooded through Reid as he froze on the spot. "I'm sorry. What?"

Gideon shrugged his shoulders. "I was wondering if you wanted me to help with anything for your wedding as well."

Reid looked to the heavens, praying for strength to make it through the next four months. He cleared his throat and turned to face Gideon. "I'm not sure who started that rumor, but it is far from the truth. I'm not dating anyone. In fact, I don't even have a date for either of the weddings."

The smile spreading across Gideon's face told Reid that he'd just stepped into Gideon's trap.

"Ahem." Gideon cleared his throat. "I know you've met my sister, Lydia. She would be a great date to take to one of the weddings. Or both, really. Let me give you her number, really quick."

Reid could feel the phone vibrating in his pocket as Gideon's text came through.

"Thanks, friend." There was no chance Reid was going to call her, but he could be polite.

The old Ford Mustang he drove was tantalizingly close. Just a few more yards through the parking lot and Reid would be free.

Luck wasn't in his favor. Lydia stepped out from behind a truck and leaned against the hood of Reid's car, her red braids hanging over her shoulders.

"I may have already told Lydia you wanted to ask her out," Gideon said. He held his hands out. "I mean, I didn't think you'd be able to tell her no."

Reid clenched his fingers into a fist. He would have welts where his nails were pressing into his palms, but he needed to stay calm.

"Hi Lydia. Can I help you with something?"

Lydia batted her eyelashes at him and giggled. "Well, I was hoping maybe we could hang out sometime."

Reid's patience was running thin. He opened his mouth to say no, but the retort died on his lips. His mom's knitting club was heading straight towards him. He had about twenty seconds to start driving or he'd have to answer to the five very animated women who loved to gossip.

"Sure, Lydia. That would be great." Reid turned the key to unlock his car. "I've really gotta go, though. Can I text you later?"

Lydia straightened up, tossing a red braid over her shoulder. "I'll be waiting by the phone."

Reid turned the key in the engine, his body relaxing as the revving of the car drowned out any more attempts at conversation. He pulled forward through a space, thanking the Lord that the person blocking him in had moved. As Reid drove out of the parking lot, he could see the dejected slump of the knitting club's shoulders.

He had dodged that bullet, but he wasn't so sure that he'd be lucky the next time.

* * *

BACK AT HOME, Reid changed out of his Sunday best and headed to the kitchen to scrounge for food. Mom Matthews would be making something delicious for dinner, but Reid knew he was going to lose his appetite as soon as the lovebirds made their appearance. Family dinners had become a bit crowded now that Emily and Hazel always joined them.

Both his mom and his youngest sister, Bree, were thrilled with everything related to the wedding. He'd often find them sitting on the couch, their heads pressed close while they oohed and aahed over dresses. If he was asked one more time which shade of blue went best with their eyes, Reid was going to explode. Blue was blue. The shade didn't matter.

Reid was reaching for a container of leftover stir fry when the front door banged shut. "We're here," Porter called.

Knowing he had about thirty seconds to clear out of the kitchen, Reid shoved the leftovers back into the fridge. He'd warm them up later when the house was empty. He reached for an apple instead and slipped out the back door as Porter and Emily's voices drew closer.

Reid's heart didn't stop thumping until he was sitting in the middle of a field, surrounded by tall stalks of grass. The cows were going to love grazing there, but for now, it was Reid's refuge from the chaos. It wasn't that he was jealous of his brothers. They were more than welcome to date and marry anyone they liked. Was it really necessary to drag him into every bit of planning though?

Finding a tuft of grass to lay back against was Reid's first order of business. He chomped on his apple while he headed to his favorite spot at the far end of the field. A small indentation in the grass showed Reid where he had spent far too much of his time. He lay back, resting his head on a tall tuft that served as a makeshift pillow.

Warm rays of sun beat down on Reid's face when he closed his eyes. If his calculations were right, he had at least an hour before anyone would start looking for him. The women would spend half that time talking about how exciting it was to be planning weddings, and the other half actually doing the planning for their special days.

Reid was drifting off to sleep when his phone began to buzz. He glanced at the number. It wasn't anyone in his contact list, so he tucked the phone back in his pocket and closed his eyes. The phone buzzed another time, but Reid wasn't interested in talking to anyone. They could leave a message if it was important. He pulled the phone out of his pocket and tossed it into the grass so the buzzing wouldn't interrupt his sleep. Then he closed his eyes and drifted off.

The sun was dipping towards the west when Reid woke up. He grabbed his phone, squinting against the glare of the sun to see that he had seventeen missed calls. Reid's stomach dropped. That many calls meant one thing. There was an emergency somewhere.

The last time Reid had gotten that many calls, he was off at college. His mom had been calling from a hospital room to tell him that his dad had passed away, but he was too busy rock climbing at the gym to pay any attention to his phone. His mom said she wasn't angry at him for missing the calls, but seven years later, Reid still felt guilty.

Tall stalks of grass whipped against Reid's jeans as he jogged through the field. He was heading home. If the emergency was somewhere else, he'd hop in the Mustang and drive to wherever he was needed.

Reid held the phone to his ear while he ran, pressing the buttons for his voicemail. The first message was from the dentist, reminding him about his upcoming appointment. The second message was from his friend Justin, asking if he could borrow one of the plows because theirs had just broken.

Reid huffed in frustration, clenching the phone in his hands while he pushed play on the next message. It was Lydia.

The sound of her whiny voice threading through the speaker brought Reid up short. He checked the number against that of the other missed calls. In a period of a couple of hours, the girl had managed to call him fifteen times. Fifteen.

Reid slowed to a walk, trying to catch his breath. There was no emergency. Instead, there was a demanding woman who didn't have any boundaries.

Each of the messages was a variation of the one before.

"Call me back," Lydia said.

"Hey, if you get this message, can you give me a call?"

"Oh, hey. Just checking if you got my last message."

"Are you ghosting me? Why haven't you called me back?"

By the time Reid got to the end of the messages, his stomach was churning. He gripped his phone as it started to vibrate.

"Hi, Lydia," Reid said. He looked around the field, trying to find something to kick, but grass surrounded him on all sides. Reid squatted down, pulling up a handful of weeds.

"Oh my gosh. You answered. And you knew it was me." Lydia's voice held all the excitement of a child experiencing Christmas for the first time. Reid guessed people didn't always take her calls.

"I was busy working on something," Reid said. He ran a hand through his hair. Did napping count as work? Reid decided it didn't matter. He had a valid reason for not answering his phone. "Did you need something?"

Lydia giggled, a high, nasally titter that caused Reid to hold the phone away from his ear. "My brother said you wanted to ask me out. My calendar is filling up quickly, so I wanted to be sure to fit you in."

"I see." Reid was going to have a few stern words with Gideon when he saw him next. There were a lot of steps between saying he'd think about asking someone out to having her call him every ten minutes.

"I told Gideon that you weren't going to call, but here we are. He was wrong."

Reid rolled his eyes. He hadn't called her, but Lydia was on a roll.

"So anyway, I'll be ready for our date tomorrow at seven. Thanks so much. Bye."

She hung up before Reid's brain connected with his mouth. How had he gotten roped into a date with Lydia? The woman hadn't given him time to answer, but he was stuck. If he said no, he'd give the town something else to gossip about. He didn't need people saying he was too good for the baker's family. The problem wasn't the family that

Lydia came from. The problem was that Reid had zero interest in settling down with anyone.

Unfortunately, it didn't matter how he felt about Lydia. Reid was already trapped. He may not have initiated the date, but he wasn't a quitter. He was going to give her the best date of her life. He had a reputation to live up to, after all. And maybe, if he took her out, his family would finally stop bothering him. How bad could one date be?

CHAPTER 2

etting stared at was a regular part of Millie's job. She spent hours each day teaching English to classrooms filled with high school students, many of whom were bored out of their minds. It didn't matter how exciting she made the lessons. There were always a handful of students who didn't seem to care what she was doing. She could be standing on her head and juggling with her feet, and she'd still be less entertaining than whatever was on their phones. They looked at her like she was speaking a language they didn't understand.

That was why, pinned under the weight of her best friend's stare, it was odd that Millie couldn't find the words to speak.

"Can you repeat the question?" Millie was stalling for time. Or for a meteor to hit. She was pretty sure her best friend Hazel had just asked her to be paired up with one of the groom's brothers for the wedding.

The bridesmaids had taken Hazel to brunch to help her

with wedding plans. Hazel and Thomas had only been engaged for a month, but the wedding was approaching fast. Neither one of them wanted to wait very long for the marriage when they had already been close friends for years. They felt like they knew each other well enough. Millie couldn't wait for them to tie the knot.

"You don't have to do much," Hazel said. "You'll just go to a few dress fittings, walk down the aisle, and sit by Reid at the reception. Maybe share a dance or two. And take some photos."

"Yeah," Steph piped in. "You'll barely notice he's there."

"And he's not bad looking at all," Dawn said. "At least your pictures will look nice."

The bridesmaids were ganging up on Millie, and she wasn't amused. "If you guys think he's such a great guy, why aren't one of you pairing up with him?" She glanced back and forth between the women.

"Been there, done that," Dawn said. "He fled our date like the police were chasing him. I swear, the guy probably doesn't even remember I exist."

"Same," Steph said. "We actually made it to three dates before he ghosted me. No phone calls. No text messages. The guy disappeared."

Hazel reached for Millie's hand. "Look. I know he's a bit of a player."

Millie held her hand up. "I don't date guys who sleep around with other women." Millie was willing to hang out with someone she didn't like if it served the greater good, but this was asking too much.

"No. He's not a player like that." Hazel pushed her

blonde hair back. "He just likes to date a lot. From what I've heard, it's never anything serious. I'm not asking you to date him. You just have to look pretty next to him, which won't be a problem for you. You're gorgeous."

Flattery was going to get her nowhere, but Millie couldn't help but smile. She was the friend that trusted too easily and was always willing to help out. That was why, when she saw Hazel's clasped hands, she knew she couldn't turn down her request.

"You know I'm only doing this because I love you, right?" Millie reached for a muffin from the basket in the center of the table and broke off a piece, tossing it into her mouth. They were seated in the corner booth of Sunny's Cafe, which was a perfect place for wedding planning. The food was delicious, and it was never too crowded.

"I know." Hazel clasped Millie's hand. "I appreciate it."

Dawn picked up a paper and waved it back and forth. "Now that the matchmaking is done . . ."

She couldn't finish her sentence because Millie growled.

"I mean, now that the, uh." Dawn took a sip of orange juice and shook her head. "I mean, now that we know who we are standing in the same vicinity of, let's see what else we can knock off this list."

The women resumed their planning, but Millie's mind couldn't focus. One silly wedding date shouldn't make a difference in her life. People paired up and broke up all the time. The real problem was that Millie had a stellar reputation she had carefully cultivated as a high school teacher. She couldn't be seen hanging out with a player.

"Did you hear me?" Steph was waving her hand in front of Millie's face.

"Sorry. What did you say?" Millie was going to have to pay better attention if she was going to be of any help.

"I asked if you had a preference of colors for your dress."

Hazel held out a ring filled with swatches of varying shades of pastel pink and purple fabric. "The dress shop makes all their gowns in these colors. I thought it would be cute if each of the groomsmen matched his tie to his bridesmaid's dress. What do you think?"

Millie tried to stay positive when she reached for the fabric. "That sounds beautiful." It was what Hazel wanted to hear, but Millie's heart was sinking. A matching tie would show the wedding guests who, exactly, Millie belonged to. How was she going to save her reputation when she was paired with the worst of the groomsmen?

With the emotions swirling through her body, Millie couldn't wait for brunch to be over. She had a stack of papers waiting to be graded at home and a week of lessons to plan. Burying herself in work would help her to forget the awkward wedding date looming in her future.

* * *

BY MONDAY MORNING, Millie had managed to convince herself that the wedding wouldn't be too bad. She had been friends with Hazel long enough to know that her friend didn't ask for favors unless it was really important to her.

Hazel was always helping people, which was why Millie knew she'd stand next to Reid no matter the cost.

Millie pulled into the parking lot, heading for the teacher's section. As she did so, she noticed the shiny new Tesla parked in Mr. Albertson's spot. This was the third new car the principal had brought to school this year.

She parked a few spaces away from the car, not wanting to get accused of scratching the Tesla's paint. Millie was heading towards the building when her friend Sheila ran to catch her. Sheila was the drama teacher at the high school. She was already starting to get a reputation through the state for the incredible quality of the plays she put on.

"Did you see the latest car?" Sheila whispered. "I know he's the principal, but how on earth does he keep affording these things?"

"Rich parents? A trust fund? A secret side hustle?" Millie wasn't sure what his secret was, but Mr. Albertson wasn't her problem for the day. "Whatever his secret, I wish he'd share it with us. Did you hear about the latest proposed budget cuts?"

Sheila groaned. "I swear, you say teacher and people start complaining. What do they think we do all day? Juggle and knit hats? Maybe if people respected us more, we'd get better funding."

Millie nodded. "It's not just the general public. It's the parents, too. Last week I had one parent complaining that I didn't assign enough homework to prepare their child for college and another parent complaining that I assigned too much busywork. I can't win."

"I get it." Sheila pulled the door open, waving Millie

through. "I'd quit, but I can't let down the kids. We're doing our final rehearsals for Mamma Mia. I'd never abandon them mid-production. This play is going to be incredible."

Millie gave her friend a quick hug. "To another day of changing lives, even if the establishment doesn't appreciate us."

"See you at lunch?" Sheila asked.

"You know it." Millie left her friend outside the drama room and headed towards the back of the school. Students were just beginning to fill the hallway. She waved at a few kids who called out her name.

This was why Millie put up with the administration. The students she taught had bright futures ahead of them. If she could give them hope, she was doing her job properly.

She was almost to the classroom when she heard her name being shouted.

"Miss Grant. Wait. Miss Grant?"

Millie didn't recognize the voice, but she turned around. Bobbing through the sea of students rushing to class was a darling girl with silky brown curls and bright blue eyes. She skidded to a stop near Millie's door, almost falling over.

"What can I do for you?" Millie asked.

The girl's face lit up. "I'm Bree Matthews. I thought Hazel was joking when she told me that one of the teachers from my school was going to be in the wedding. Then I looked you up online. You really are a teacher here."

Bree's enthusiasm was infectious but neither one of them had time to be lingering in the hallway. Millie glanced at her watch. The bell was going to ring in less than a minute. Still, she was curious about the sister of the infamous Reid. "I'm glad you found me. What grade are you in?"

"I'm a junior. I can't wait to be a senior though. Maybe I'll take a class from you next year." Bree waved at a group of boys walking by and Millie hid a smile. Maybe the sister was a little more like her brother than anyone thought.

As long as Bree didn't come with her brother attached, that was fine by Millie. "It was great to meet you. I'd better get to class, but I'm sure I'll see you around."

"You're coming to the dress shop this Saturday, right?"

Millie smacked her forehead. She had been so busy stressing about the dress fitting, she had completely forgotten to put it on her calendar. So much for keeping an organized schedule. "Thanks for the reminder, Bree. I'll see you there."

The bell was ringing when Millie stepped into the classroom.

"Cutting it close, Miss G," Derek called out. He was one of the more popular students in the school. More than one girl had written about him during their creative writing assignments.

"You didn't think I'd miss class, did you?" Millie locked her purse in a desk drawer and then headed to the front of the room.

The students were attentively watching her, waiting for class to begin.

"Last week we talked about the hero of the story. That

person is called . . .?" She trailed off, waiting for the class to answer in unison.

"The protagonist."

"Exactly." Millie had done her job well. "The protagonist is the person you want to root for in the story."

A petite girl in the third row raised her hand high.

"Yes, Sophia?"

"I have my protagonist figured out. Can I start working on my story?"

Millie shook her head. "Not yet. We aren't quite done with the unit yet. If the protagonist is someone we want to root for in the book, does anyone know what the opposite character would be."

"The bad guy."

"The jerk of the story."

"The evil stepmother."

"The guy that ends up in jail."

The students clamored over one another while Millie wrote each idea on the board. From the middle of the chaos, she heard a small voice say, "My dad."

Ice water doused Millie's spirits. She was teaching a classroom full of students who came from some of the most upstanding families in the town, but it was easy to forget that some of those students were living lives that most people couldn't dream of.

She wanted to spin around and ask the students who said their dad, but she knew better. Instead, she continued to write the ideas on the board. While she wrote, she said a silent prayer that someone would be able to help the girl who was struggling.

After gathering her thoughts, Millie turned back to the class. "Thanks for that great list. All of these are examples of an antagonist. Who can tell me why we need an antagonist in the story?"

"For conflict?" Derek called.

"Exactly. Good versus evil. Right versus wrong. Even man versus nature."

Sophia's hand waved in the air. "Nature isn't a person."

"You're right. The antagonist doesn't always have to be a person. It can be a situation or a natural disaster that keeps the protagonist from reaching their goals. We'll talk more about the varieties of antagonists tomorrow. Today, we're going to free-write for a half hour. Create a character for me that can exist in society without being obviously evil. I don't want to read about any Darth Vader or Voldemort types. I want someone more subtle."

"Are we turning these in?" Derek asked.

"You are. No names. We're going to trade papers and analyze them to see if we can find any common traits."

There was a small amount of chatter, but the students soon settled down to work on their assignment. Millie opened her own document and wrote alongside her students. When the timer beeped Millie felt much better. Her antagonist had started as a man who couldn't commit to a relationship if his life depended on it. It slowly morphed into a boss who was embezzling money from the company. No one would recognize the principal, Mr. Albertson, as the villain, but Millie knew who she meant.

There was a reason she loved creative writing. By the time the bell rang, signaling the end of class, Millie's mind was clear. She was going to make it through the wedding, and she was going to uncover the mystery behind Mr. Albertson's constant car upgrades. That was what a good protagonist would do.

The rest of the week flew by. Her creative writing class was still discussing the antagonist of a story, but they were learning how to flesh out the villain. It was easy to write about someone who was clearly evil. What if the person was misguided instead? The latest batch of essays showed a lot of potential from the students.

The weekend found Millie curled up on her couch, a red pen in hand while she graded papers. She was partway through a story involving a three headed spider when she got a text from Hazel asking her where she was. A quick glance at the time sent a wave of panic though her. Millie had gotten so caught up in reading the papers, she totally lost track of time.

I'm on my way, she texted before dashing to her car. She sped through yellow lights to shave off a few seconds, only to come to a standstill when she hit Main Street. Not surprisingly, for a Saturday morning, there wasn't an open parking spot in sight. She was cursing her bad luck when a car parked across the street from her put on their reverse lights. Millie flipped on her turn signal, crossing her fingers that she'd be able to make it across oncoming traffic in time.

She was making a U-turn at the light when a Ford Mustang came barreling up beside her, passing her on the left. The car cut her off and snaked into Millie's open spot before she could turn on her blinkers.

There was nothing left to do but circle the block again. A tall, dark-haired man was shutting the door of the car when Millie drove by. He fit the description of a gorgeous protagonist, but Millie shook her fist at him. Men who stole parking spaces weren't heroes. They were villains. And everyone knew that the handsome villains were the worst kind.

Millie ended up parking three blocks away from the bridal shop. The wind picked up as she ran to the shop. By the time she pulled open the door, the room was filled with people. The wedding party turned to stare at her when the jingling of the bell above the door announced her arrival.

"I'm so glad you could make it," Hazel said, stepping to Millie's side. She pulled Millie into a hug so she could whisper in her ear. "You might want to fix your hair."

Millie glanced at her reflection in the shop window and held back a groan. Her nicely styled bun now resembled a bird's nest, with strands of hair sticking out at the top. She pulled her scrunchie out, letting her black hair fall around her shoulders before she curled it back into a bun.

Hazel tugged Millie's hand, pulling her to join the group. "Evelyn was just matching up the bridesmaids and groomsmen so we can coordinate your dress and tie colors. I'll be standing at the front of the wedding party with this handsome man." She nudged Thomas in the ribs, and he rewarded her with a grin. "Porter and Emily are going to be next in line."

The love in Porter's eyes was apparent when he looked at Emily. Millie felt a twinge of jealousy, but she pushed it to the side. She turned her focus instead on the parking space thief. Some unlucky woman was going to have to stand next to him for the night. Maybe being paired with the player wasn't the worst thing that could happen. At least he wasn't rude.

Bree appeared by her side. "Isn't this exciting?"

"You're over here, Bree." Hazel was still playing matchmaker. Bree hurried off to her spot before Millie could answer.

The pit in Millie's stomach sank as she watched the row of groomsmen dwindling smaller. The more she looked, the more obvious the family resemblance became. The parking space thief was most definitely related to the groom. He had the same dark hair, but his eyes were a vibrant shade of green.

Millie had heard gossip about how handsome the Matthews family brothers were but seeing them lining up in a row left little to dispute. She now understood where the rumors came from. She was studying the men to look for other resemblances when Hazel cleared her throat.

"Did you hear me?" Hazel asked.

Millie shook her head. "Sorry. I was distracted. What did you say?"

Hazel pointed to the parking thief, who was tousling Bree's hair. "I was saying that you'll be standing next to Reid."

As Reid's green eyes met hers, Millie spoke the words on her mind. "Anyone want to trade?"

CHAPTER 3

Reid rubbed his ear. He was hearing things wrong because it sounded an awful lot like the woman in front of him was looking to trade partners.

"Why would you want to do that?" Reid asked. He held out his hand to shake hers. "I'm the fun brother."

Millie's eyebrows shot up as she shook his hand. "I know who you are. We'll have to wait and see about the fun part."

"If you already know who I am, why would you possibly want to swap for someone else?" Reid ignored Millie's angry eyes, telling himself that she must be mad about something else, because he hadn't been there long enough to annoy anyone yet. "Have I already done something to mess up?"

"You really don't know?"

Reid shook his head. "Nope. I arrived a little late but so did you. That shouldn't make a difference."

"I was only late because I had trouble finding a parking

spot. Some jerk cut me off when I was turning to get it." Millie raised her brows. "Any idea who that could be?"

His stomach started churning. "Let me see. I'm guessing it was me?" He didn't need to start an argument with Millie, no matter how primed she seemed to be for a fight.

"Yep." The pop she added to the end of her word enunciated her annoyance. Women seemed to get that way around Reid. He had been told he was a bit much to handle over the years, but it seemed a bit premature for Millie to already be upset.

No matter the problem, this was Thomas's special day. Really, it was probably Hazel's idea to have the bridal party paired up. In the end it didn't matter why they had to have partners. Reid's only job was to be there with a smile on his face. He wasn't going to let this temperamental woman mess it up.

"Clearly, I couldn't see that you were coming. Then again, I don't know how I could miss someone as pretty as you." He held his hand out, waiting for Millie to shake it. "I'm genuinely sorry. Truce?"

The blue eyes that fixed on him took his breath away. She smirked, which caused a dimple to appear on one cheek. "You do know I'm a teacher, right?"

It was a strange segue, but Reid went with it. "Sure. That vaguely rings a bell. You teach at the high school?"

"Yep. That means I get lied to on a daily basis. Sometimes it is simple, like the typical dog at my homework sort of stuff. Other times it is more elaborate."

There was probably a point to the rambling. If there

was, Reid was lost. Maybe Millie was on to something asking to trade dates. She seemed a little unhinged.

"I've got a pretty good sense of detecting when people are telling the truth."

"I see. So, what do you sense when you talk to me?"

Millie looked up as her name was called to join the women on the other side of the shop.

"Honestly, I'm not sure."

Millie walked away, leaving Reid standing alone in the middle of the store. He shook his head once to bring his focus back to the room. Feeling centered again, he walked to his brother Porter's side.

"You're lucky," he said, whispering out of the side of his mouth while he held his arms out to his side. The tailor held a measuring tape across his back, pausing to jot down notes.

"How so?" Porter asked. He turned his back to Reid holding his arms down while he was measured.

"You don't have to think about who to take to the wedding. You have Emily."

Porter's eyes got soft when he turned to face Reid. "She is something special."

The pang of jealousy reared its head again. Reid scowled, pushing his thoughts away. If anyone deserved a good life, it was his brother, Porter. Loss changed people, and yet Porter somehow managed to trust in love again after burying his first wife. There was a tenderness to Porter's voice when he talked about Emily. He knew how fleeting life could be, and he seemed to cherish his relationship much deeper than most people gave him credit for.

Reid wasn't ready for that kind of a commitment. It didn't help that the women he dated all seemed to be a bit on the unstable side. Take Lydia. He had taken her out to dinner at Clucks and Fries, a local diner. She was fine when they were ordering food but by the time dessert rolled around, she was talking about marriage and how many kids they were going to have. Why couldn't women understand that he wasn't looking for that sort of a relationship? He had a ranch to run. That didn't exactly allow time to look for a wife.

Reid was happy for his brother, but not pleased with his own predicament. "Well, I've been paired with someone who is already mad at me."

Porter's eyes crinkled. "How did you manage that?"

"I'm not sure. Something to do with a parking space. At least all I have to do is stand next to her and look good. That is something I can handle." He lifted his arm to flex his muscles, causing the tailor to scold him.

"Sorry." Reid held back a laugh as he lowered his arms. If the day kept unfolding how it had been, he was going to be in trouble every time he opened his mouth. It wasn't a great end to the week.

Porter smirked, "You have to be able to dance with her, too. You heard about the dance number the wedding party is doing, right?"

Reid froze in place. "You've got to be kidding me."

"Sadly, I'm not. I guess it's always been Hazel's dream to have one of those silly dances."

"But . . . Thomas doesn't dance." Reid's stomach was swirling with nerves. His brother could outrun and angry bull, but he tripped over his own feet when trying to dance. That idea had disaster written all over it.

Porter shrugged. "Hey. If Thomas wants to humiliate himself in front of a crowd, more power to him. It's not like picking up the dance will be difficult for you."

That was true. Reid had taken a few social dance classes back in college. That didn't make the idea of dancing with Millie any easier to stomach. He needed to get out of the wedding shop before he said something judgmental that he'd regret.

Reid tapped his foot, waiting for Hazel to approve his tie choice. As soon as he got her approval, he muttered some excuse about needing to get back to the ranch. The fresh air outside helped to clear Reid's mind. He sucked in a couple of deep breaths, letting the air course through his body as he debated what to do next. Any task sounded better than getting fitted for a suit.

Thinking through the tasks on the ranch gave Reid the idea he needed. There was a lock on one of the barn doors that had rusted shut. A quick trip to the hardware store for the proper oil would clear his mind.

Reid's mood lifted when he pulled into the parking lot. He wandered up and down the aisles, stopping to check out the latest gadgets. The oil he needed was towards the back of the store. It took all his willpower to leave behind the power saw section, but they already had more tools than the ranch needed. The family didn't need the newest or shiniest tools to get the job done.

He was rounding the corner when he smacked into something solid. Stepping back, the apology died on his lips when he saw who he had run into. Lydia was standing with her cart in the middle of the aisle, wrestling with a large board.

Stomach dropping, Reid stepped forward. "Let me help you with that," he said, easing the board onto the cart.

"You're my hero," Lydia gushed. "What are the odds of running into you here? I wasn't sure when I'd see you again after our date, but I guess fate had other plans."

Reid's eyes darted down the aisle, looking for anything he could grab. "It's a strange coincidence." He reached for a measuring tape that was hanging near the boards, trying to make an excuse for why he was there. "That's what I was looking for. I'd better be on my way."

Lydia opened her eyes wide and batted her lashes at him. Reid thought that was only something people did in cartoons. Did she actually think she was making herself more attractive? The question was answered when she fluffed her hair and pushed her lips out into a pout.

"I just need a few more things." Lydia waved her list at Reid. "You could help me shop if you wanted. Kind of like a mini second date."

Reid held the measuring tape out in front of him. "Sorry. No time. I've got a few things I need to take care of on the ranch."

He ducked past, avoiding arms that were reaching out for a hug. So much for the store being a good distraction.

* * *

Things began to look better once Reid got back home. If he was away from people, there was no way he could manage to get himself in trouble. Instead, he made his way to the kitchen to fill his water bottle before he headed out to the fields.

Reid propped open the back door so fresh air could circulate through the house. Spring was his favorite season. Cold temperatures finally were relaxing their grip on the land, which made working on the ranch much more enjoyable.

He was tightening the lid on his water bottle when the doorbell rang. Reid opened the front door and tried to stifle a laugh. The man on the porch was covered head to toe in a light cream powder. His attempts to wipe the powder off his face had left him with rings around his eyes.

"Hard day?" Reid asked.

The driver nodded. "Embarrassing, more than anything. I pulled out my knife to cut the plastic off your delivery and I managed to knick the edge of one of the formula bags. It exploded all over my truck. And me."

Reid covered his mouth, trying to hide his snicker. "Sorry, man."

The driver started laughing. "It's really quite the rookie mistake. We'll get you a replacement and throw in an extra bag for free. I'm so sorry about that."

"Mistakes happen." Reid pulled up his delivery list. "That was formula for our calves. We had a couple who got rejected by their mom." He pulled on his boots and followed the driver to the truck.

"Yep. It was the worst bag to knick."

Light cream flakes of dried formula had formed a small pile, which had then been trampled through by the driver. The bag was no longer spilling, but the damage had been done. It was going to take forever to clean up the mess from every corner of the truck.

"I'm glad you were my last delivery, or I'd have had some pretty annoyed customers. No one ordered a special coating of powder with their deliveries."

"I get it. How can I help?" Reid knew the driver was going to need a pallet jack to pull out the pallets. That wasn't going to work so well with a mound of dry formula in the way.

"You got a big broom?"

It took just a couple of minutes to sweep most of the mess out of the truck onto the ground, and another couple of minutes to direct the driver where to put the order. As Reid worked, he had the nagging suspicion that something was off in the kitchen. He hadn't meant to leave the door open for so long, but what was the worst that could happen? Too many flies might get inside but that was to be expected on a ranch.

As soon as the last of the pallets were delivered, Reid headed back to the kitchen. If he remembered correctly, most of the wedding party was heading out for lunch. He needed to grab his water bottle and some snacks so he could stay out in the fields for a good part of the afternoon. That way he'd get to miss all the wedding chatter.

Reid pushed open the kitchen door and froze. As he stood there, his brain struggled to process the chaos that was unfolding before him. The chickens, who had contentedly been looking for bugs on the far back lawn, had apparently decided they were ready to be domesticated. At least a dozen of them had wandered into the kitchen, strutting around as if they owned the place.

The situation was so absurd, Reid wasn't sure what to do. Then he remembered his priorities. He whipped out his phone to snap a picture, because no one was going to believe him. Then it was time for some chicken wrangling.

It was easy to chase the first chicken down, gently pinning her wings to her side while he escorted her to the back door. He set her down and carefully closed the door behind him so he could repeat the task without any chickens wandering back in.

Half the chickens were back outside where they belonged when Reid noticed a big problem. The remainder of the chickens were happily pecking at a pile of fabric. On closer inspection, he realized they were pecking at sequins and beads, scratching their claws across the sheer fabric.

Reid clutched his stomach, his heart dropping. That wasn't a random piece of fabric that the chickens were playing with. It was a veil. A now dirty, somewhat ripped, chicken-pecked veil. One of his brothers was going to kill him. Or rather, one of their fiancés.

Reid sank to his knees, shooing the chickens off while he gathered the veil in his arms. He vaguely remembered a conversation between Hazel and his mom about getting it ready for the ceremony. The memory flooded back, bringing bile to Reid's throat. Hazel had an heirloom veil, which had been passed down from her grandma to her mom. Now it was passing to her.

Reid was in trouble.

He set the veil on the table and lunged for another chicken. It didn't take long to get the rest of them out of the house, but the damage had been done. There was no way he could recover from this mess.

* * *

REID WAS LYING under his truck, doing a basic oil change, when the crunch of car wheels on the gravel told him that the family was home. He gulped, debating if it would be better to stay under the truck instead of facing the music. That was the cowardly thing to do, though, and he wasn't a coward. Instead, he quickly tightened the bolt he was working on and slid out from beneath the truck, wiping his hands on a rag.

When he saw Millie walking to the door, he almost ducked back under the truck. She wasn't the family he was expecting. She knocked on the door, and then, when no one answered, she pulled her hair out of its bun, letting the beautiful dark waves cascade down her shoulders. She was twisting her hair back up when Reid called out.

Millie yelped, and spun around, grabbing the handrail for balance.

"It's rude manners to sneak up on a person." She had fire in her eyes as her hands flew to her hips. "Why would you do that?"

"You're knocking on the door, right? How else am I supposed to answer it?"

"How can you answer it if you're outside?" She waved behind her, in the general direction of the door without taking her eyes off Reid.

He took a step back. The woman was clearly a bit unhinged if she couldn't understand why a cowboy would be outside his house. Did she honestly think that he should be stuck inside? She obviously had never been to a ranch before.

"It really isn't any of your business why I am inside or out of my house, is it? Now, can I help you with something? I thought you all were eating lunch somewhere." Reid wanted to push past the woman to go inside and wash his hands properly, but she didn't look like she was going to budge.

"Everyone is heading home. They had to stop at the fabric store really quick."

Reid wanted to throw up. His entire family would be around to watch as Hazel discovered her veil. He had to get to the kitchen and hide the evidence, but first he had to wash the grease off his hands. The last thing he needed was to add black smudges to the veil.

"Got it. They should be back soon. Do you want to come inside and wait?"

Millie's expression wasn't difficult to read as she looked him up and down, her eyes landing on a spot of oil on his shirt. "It looks like you were in the middle of something?"

"Oil change. I was just finishing up." Reid pushed open the door and led the way into the family room. "You can wait here." There were plenty of couches for Millie to choose from.

"If you're thirsty, kitchen's through there. And the bathroom is just around the corner. I'd say make yourself at home, but somehow, I have the feeling you already will, being a teacher and all."

That earned a laugh, highlighting the dimples on Millie's cheeks. "Thanks, Reid."

Reid took the stairs to his room, stopping at the bathroom on the way to scrub every speck of oil off his hands. Once they were clean, he headed to his closet to grab a new shirt. He was reaching for a ripped t-shirt when he remembered who was sitting in his family room. The teacher was already marking him down for stealing her spot. She didn't need to judge him for wearing old clothes, too.

He grabbed a maroon t-shirt out of the closet and was pulling it over his head when a horrified scream echoed through the house. Feet thudding down the steps, Reid's heart raced while he ran to see what was wrong. The scream had to come from Millie, but what trouble could she have possibly gotten into? She seemed competent enough to be left alone. It took just a few seconds for Reid's brain to catch up.

There was one thing in the house that would bring out that kind of a reaction. Millie must have found the veil. He clenched his fists, bracing himself for what he'd find when he walked into the kitchen.

Millie was standing with her back to the door, holding in her hands the source of Reid's stomach ache. He watched as she tried to smooth down the lace, failing with each attempt.

"There was an accident," Reid said. He cleared his throat. "It couldn't be helped."

Millie spun to face him, holding the veil in one hand. "What did you do to this?"

Reid rolled his shoulders back. "It wasn't me. It was the chickens."

"The . . . chickens?" Millie ran her fingers down a section of the veil, trying to press the lace back down. "You do know you've ruined Hazel's wedding, right?"

What was Reid supposed to say to that? It wasn't like he had been trying to let the chickens in. He couldn't have predicted the chain of events if he tried. "Like I said. It was an accident."

Millie set the veil back on the table and walked to the sink. She was so quiet washing her hands, Reid assumed she was gearing up for a big lecture. Sure enough, there was fire in her eyes when she turned to face him.

"How are you going to fix this?"

Reid rocked back on his heels. He already knew he was going to be in deep trouble with his brother. He didn't have to stand by and listen to a lecture from the woman he had met hours earlier.

"It isn't any of your business, is it?" Reid grabbed the veil off the table. He wasn't going to explain himself to her but seeing her wash her hands had given him an idea. If he could at least clean up a little muck from the edges, maybe the veil wouldn't look so bad.

CHAPTER 4

*T*here was no doubt in Millie's mind that she had stepped into an alternate universe because Reid was heading towards the kitchen sink with the veil in his hands.

"What are you doing?" The horrified look on her face should have been enough to stop Reid in his tracks, but he was still reaching for the faucet.

"I'm trying to wash the dirt off." Reid held the long veil up, which made the grime even more visible.

"That part doesn't look like dirt." Millie pointed to a large clump.

"Yeah. I'm pretty sure chicken poop isn't going to go over well with the bride-to-be."

Millie watched in horror as he turned on the faucet and dunked the veil into the water.

"What if it ruins the fabric?"

Reid turned to look over his shoulder, his eyebrow raised. "Compared to what, exactly?"

The guy had a point. "You're right, I guess. But wouldn't a dry cleaner be better?"

He turned back to the sink. "I didn't think of that. It's too late now, though."

The desire to leave the kitchen and wait in the family room was a strong one. Millie didn't want to be anywhere near Reid when Hazel caught him. She was heading towards the door when her sense of loyalty kicked in. The veil certainly wasn't her problem, but how could she walk away? She would do anything she could to make things better for Hazel.

"I can't believe I'm saying this, but what can I do to help?" Millie waited for Reid to turn around. As she did, she took a moment to study the man. He had changed out of the greasy shirt he had been wearing when she arrived into a soft maroon t-shirt, which hugged his broad shoulders. The man wasn't bulked out, but she could see the outline of lean muscles that Reid must have built up working on the ranch.

Millie was starting to examine his other assets when his body shifted sideways. It took a second to realize what he was reaching for. "You're going to put dish soap on it?" Somehow that felt very wrong.

"Again. At this point, does it really matter?" He paused, as if he was actually waiting for Millie's permission to proceed.

Millie looked into his eyes and huffed. "You're right. Scoot over and let me help."

Reid stepped to the side and handed Millie a section of fabric. "This part is pretty bad. Are you going to be able to handle it?"

"I've seen worse." Millie squirted a little bit of dish soap onto the veil and began to rub, trying not to think about what she was touching. She was doing it to help Hazel. After a minute, the chicken poop began to slough off, leaving behind the sheer tulle fabric. He had been right about the dish soap.

Next to her, Reid was getting similar results. "I can't believe this is actually working."

"Yeah. You're extremely lucky. Are you ready to rinse it?"

Reid nodded.

Millie gently set the veil in the sink, holding just the very top of it. She slowly gathered the clean part of the veil in her arms as Reid rinsed the suds off. By the time they were done, her hands were full. The veil was wet, but it looked much better.

"I'll be back in a second." Reid ran out of the kitchen. He came back with an armful of towels. "Let's dry this off."

Amazingly, the veil looked even better once it started to dry. "One problem down, one to go." Reid looked entirely too pleased with himself.

It was time to give the cowboy a reality check. Millie pointed to a large gash in the fabric. It was surrounded by dozens of smaller slits. "You did the easy part. Any ideas on how to fix the tears?" She couldn't wait to hear his answer.

"My mom taught me to sew when I was little. I'm sure I can handle a few patches."

"This isn't the same as repairing a hole in a pair of jeans. The netting will show every stitch."

Reid frowned. "You're right. I'm stumped."

Millie was used to having an answer for everything, but even she was drawing a blank. How did people fix tears when the thread was thicker than the fabric itself? It was time to consult an expert.

She was reading an article about restoring old veils when the front door opened, and voices filled the house.

Reid started to wad the veil into a ball but then he stopped. "May as well face the music," he said.

Even though she hadn't been at fault at all, Millie felt like a child who had just gotten caught breaking a vase. She glanced at Reid. Instead of shirking away from the truth, he was standing with his shoulders back as he faced the door. The guy may be a heartbreaker, but at least he was an honest one.

"Where is everyone?" The sound of footsteps echoed down the hall.

"We're in the kitchen," Reid called.

Millie thought she could detect a slight tremble in his voice. She was tempted to step in front of him and hide the veil from Hazel's eyes, but Reid was right. It was time to fess up. She actually felt bad for the guy.

Porter and Emily were the first to enter the kitchen. He raised an eyebrow at his brother, but then he walked past, heading for the fridge.

Thomas and Hazel were laughing when they came in with Mom Matthews, but their smiles fell when Reid stepped forward with the veil.

Hazel's hand flew to her mouth. "I can't believe it. What did you guys do?"

Reid cleared his throat. "I had a little incident with the chickens."

"The chickens?" Hazel looked at Millie. "What is he talking about?"

It was time to make a decision. Millie could side with Reid, helping to defend his actions, or she could throw him to the wolves. So far Hazel hadn't been a bridezilla, but there was always time for that personality to come out. Millie didn't want to tempt fate. She took a deep breath, ready to confess, but Reid shook his head at her before she could speak.

"Don't blame her." Reid squared his shoulders. "It was all me."

"You cleaned my veil all by yourself?" Hazel took the veil from his hands and held it out in front of her, the fabric dropping almost to the ground. "It looks so much better."

The way the veil was hanging, it was obvious that there was a large tear right down the center of it. They had seconds before Hazel would see it.

Mom Matthews lifted an edge of the veil. "Tell the truth, Reid. Did Millie help you?" She was running her hand down the lace.

So much for being off the hook. Millie wasn't going to let the guy flounder any longer. "I did. It was much easier washing it with two people."

Hazel flung her arms around Millie and Reid. "You guys are amazing."

Millie glanced sideways at Reid. Were they hearing the same thing?

"I'm sorry about the tear," Reid said. His body tensed next to Millie's.

Hazel dropped her arms. "The tear?" She held the veil up, tracing the jagged edge with her fingers. Her voice grew soft. "My mom put that tear in the veil when she was leaving for her honeymoon. She was turning to wave goodbye to her friends when it got caught on a jagged piece of a fence. That's why I brought the veil here."

"I'm going to help her transfer the lace to a new piece of tulle." Mom Matthews put her arm around Hazel's shoulders. "That way you'll have something old and something new when you walk down the aisle."

Millie glanced at Reid, who was working hard to keep a straight face. "How sweet." She had about two seconds before she was going to lose it. "I, uh, left something in the car."

"I'm going to help her get it," Reid said.

They made it to the front door before Millie busted up, doubling over with laughter. "Do you ever play the lottery?"

Reid was shaking with laughter beside her. "Nope. Why?"

"Because I'm pretty sure you're the luckiest guy in the world. I can't believe you got out of that."

Reid's smile fell. "You were willing to take the blame with me." He looked at Millie, and the butterflies that she made her students read about in school began to flutter in her stomach. He had a sincerity in his eyes that shot right to her core.

"Why is that?"

Millie reached for her necklace and slid the charm back and forth. "Hazel is going to be your sister-in-law. I didn't want her to have a reason to hate you."

"What about you?" His eyes were genuine; the mischievous sparkle fading away as if Reid actually cared what she thought.

"What about me?" Millie needed to get back to the safety of the kitchen. It was obvious why Reid was known for breaking hearts. His green eyes were a forest that someone could easily get lost in. He was a little too handsome for his own good.

"Do you still have a reason to hate me?" Reid angled his body towards hers, not breaking eye contact.

Millie opened her mouth but quickly closed it again. "The jury's still out, cowboy."

* * *

IT TOOK the rest of the weekend, but by the time school started on Monday, Millie had put Reid out of her mind. She didn't need the image of Reid's silly grin while he held the veil to keep popping into her thoughts whenever she had a quiet moment. Reid was her date for the wedding, and that was it. She headed to her final class of the day, eager to start a new creative writing unit.

Bree Matthews was standing by the doorway, waiting for Millie. "Did you have fun at the dress fitting?" She was bouncing up and down. "The dresses are going to be gorgeous."

"They really are. I'd love to talk about our dresses, but

don't you have class? The bell is going to ring any second." Millie didn't want Bree to get in the habit of being late.

"It's just a couple of doors down. Reid wanted me to give you this." She held out a yellow piece of paper that had been folded into a small square.

Millie reached for the paper, her stomach fluttering when she saw her name scribbled on the front in the center of a flower. Who passed notes these days? It had to be a joke.

"Thanks, Bree." She took the note and headed into the classroom, setting it to the side of her desk. She wanted to read it, but first she had a class to teach.

"Last week we spent some time with the antagonists of the story. We now have our two main characters. The protagonist and the antagonist. Is that all we need for a good story?"

Hands shot up around the classroom. A half hour later, the students were quietly working on a list of supporting characters who would help bring their stories to life. Millie gave it a moment to make sure the class was really settled before she headed to her desk.

The yellow note taunted her from the side where she had set it. If she were smart, she'd wait to open the note until class was over. Her focus was supposed to be on the students. Then again, they were all engaged at the moment. Curiosity won the battle.

Reid's handwriting was messy, but Millie had years of practice deciphering poor penmanship. The message was short, but it made Millie giggle. She clasped a hand over her mouth to keep from laughing out loud and disturbing the students.

Dear Teacher,

I'm sorry for making a mess of the veil.

Thanks for helping me to clean it up.

Yours truly,

The Cowboy

At the bottom of the letter was a small picture of two stick figures holding a long square between them. Reid had written their names above each figure and had drawn an arrow to the rectangle that was labeled "sad, sad wedding veil".

The very bottom of the paper had a small question. *Do you forgive me? Check yes or no.*

Millie couldn't hide the smile on her face. How was she supposed to stay mad at the guy when he was so ridiculous? She picked up a pen, hovering between the two boxes. "Who am I kidding?" she whispered. She knew what her answer would be. She checked a box and folded the paper back up, watching the clock until the bell rang.

Bree was waiting outside the door where the students filed out. "Did you read the note?"

Millie held it out. "Your brother is a nut, but yes, I did."

"So, what box did you check?" Bree was bouncing on her toes again.

"Hey, did you read my super-secret note?" Millie wasn't surprised. She probably would have been too curious to hand it over without taking a peek herself.

Bree's smile creased her eyes as she reached into her pocket. "Nope. Well, Reid showed me the note before he folded it up." She held out two more papers. "I'm supposed to give you the right note for whatever box you checked. Personally, I hope you picked yes. I'm not sure what my brother is apologizing for, but he's a good guy."

"What if I checked both boxes? Can I get both notes?" Millie was curious what the cowboy had to say for himself.

"Reid was pretty specific. You can just pick one. And I have to trade. Once you give me his note, I can give you the new one." Bree waved at one of her friends walking by before turning back to Millie. "So, what did you choose?"

Millie held out the yellow paper. "I said yes. I would forgive him."

"Yay!" Bree was bouncing up and down on her tiptoes when she held the note out. "I hope you guys have fun."

That was cryptic. "Thanks, Bree." Millie held the new note close to her chest, ready to tear it open once Bree had left. She waited until Bree was around the corner before stepping back into her now empty classroom.

The note was on blue paper this time with the word yes scribbled on both sides. It looked like Reid really didn't want Bree to be able to mix them up. Millie's hands trembled when she unfolded the paper and ran her hand over it to remove any creases.

I hoped you'd say yes. It would be awful if you were mad at me during the wedding.

Millie agreed. The guy deserved points for being perceptive.

I'd like to get to know you better. How about dinner this evening?

There was a stack of papers on Millie's desk waiting to

be graded and she had a quiz to prepare. She was drowning in responsibilities, but she picked up her phone and sent a short text message.

Yes to dinner.

Reid's reply came through quickly. **Pick you up from school at five?**

Millie hit the thumbs up button and threw her phone on her desk as if it were on fire. What had she done? Had she really just agreed to go out with Mr. Heartbreak himself? Only time would tell if that was a good idea or a terrible one.

CHAPTER 5

The text message on his phone said yes, but Reid had to check it a couple of times to make sure it was actually there. Sending a folded paper note to Millie like a third grader had been a risk. His brothers had teased him about it all evening, but Bree said it would be cute. In the end, the risk had paid off because now he had a date to get ready for.

Reid tucked his phone in his pocket and turned his attention back to the field he was plowing. It was almost time to plant if they were going to take advantage of the late spring harvest. The entire family would pitch in to help with the actual planting, but Reid was taking care of the prep work.

Leaving a field half plowed went against all of Reid's instincts, but when his alarm went off, he turned off the tractor and headed for home. He'd have to wake up early tomorrow to stay on track, but it was worth it if Millie was willing to give him the time of day.

There wasn't time for much more than a quick shower, but Reid took his time to style his hair before he left the bathroom. He'd already made a couple of bad first impressions. It was time to make a good one. He was pulling on his boots when Porter appeared in the doorway to his bedroom.

"Heading out, little brother?"

Reid's stomach sank. He knew what was coming. "Where's the darn belt?" The question came out more like a demand.

The tradition to wear an awful gold belt buckle on first dates was something he started. When he won the giant belt buckle at the fair as a kid, he thought it was the coolest thing ever. The large oval buckle featured bulls locking horns. He wore it proudly to school, even though it went halfway up his stomach. His teacher told him to leave it home the next day because it was causing too many distractions.

When they grew older, what started as a joke became a sort of test for the women the brothers dated. You could tell a lot about a woman based on her reaction to it.

Reid had been more than willing to put on the belt over the years, when he really didn't care about his dates. Now he was regretting ever winning the thing. Between the accidental parking theft and the veil fiasco with the chickens, Millie was already holding a bit of a grudge. This was going to be a third strike against him, and he barely knew the woman.

Thomas joined Porter and blocked the doorway, the belt hanging from his hands. "Do you need some help putting it on?" He was laughing, but Reid knew his brothers weren't above tackling him to the ground if they needed to.

"Hand it over." Reid took the belt from Thomas and headed to his room, slamming the door in his face. As the brother who liked to date the most, Reid knew exactly which shirt would compliment the gold of the belt. He always said that if the belt didn't scare the girl away, she was worth a second date. It was a silly theory, but both Hazel and Emily had passed the test and now they were engaged to his brothers.

Reid didn't know where that line of thought was coming from. He certainly wasn't looking for a forever companion. The date tonight was simply a peace offering to thank Millie for her help earlier and to apologize once again for cutting her off. If he could make a better impression, maybe standing next to the woman at the wedding wouldn't be too bad.

Mom Matthews was waiting at the bottom of the stairs, holding her phone in front of her.

"You've got to be kidding me," Reid muttered. He jutted his hip to the side and tucked his thumbs under the belt, grinning for his mom while she snapped a picture.

"Have fun tonight," she said.

"You do realize Millie may never speak to me again, right? If that happens, I'm not taking the blame for ruining Thomas and Hazel's wedding."

Mom Matthews tucked her phone into her back pocket. "If Millie is the type of woman I think she is, you're going to be just fine."

"I guess we'll find out soon enough." Reid kissed his mom's cheek and headed out the door, telling himself that nerves were to be expected. He was a diplomat on a peace mission. That was all. Sometimes you had to meet with the enemy to negotiate peace.

Halfway down the freeway, Reid realized his mistake. He had offered to pick Millie up at the school. A gentleman wouldn't exactly pull into the bus lane and honk the horn. He was going to have to march around the high school wearing a ridiculous belt with a buckle the size of a small child's face. It was late in the day, but there would still be plenty of students milling around, doing their various after school activities. Hopefully they wouldn't give their teacher a hard time.

When Reid pulled into the school parking lot, his hands began to shake. It was one thing to wear a silly belt on a date with someone he didn't really care about. It was something different to wear the belt on a peace mission. He was reaching to undo the belt buckle when he saw Bree running towards his car. She would tattle if she caught him without the buckle. He was stuck.

Reid was climbing out of the car when Bree and her friends began to applaud.

"I told them you'd wear it," she said. "You look ridiculous. I love it."

"Thanks, sis." Reid tipped his hat towards Bree's friends, winking at her best friend Madison, who held her phone up. If he was lucky, she was just taking a photo. Knowing Madison, she was probably filming the entire thing.

"Smile for the camera," Madison said. "I do have your permission to post this, right?"

Reid groaned. It didn't matter what he said. Mads was going to post it anyway.

"Anyone want to show me where Miss Grant's classroom is?" Belt buckle or not, Reid was going to pick up Millie at her door like a proper gentleman.

"I have her for creative writing," Derek said.

He stepped to the front of the group and led the way through hallways lined with lockers and motivational posters. The school smelled faintly of sweat mixed with perfume from the students. Things hadn't really changed since Reid was a student twelve years ago.

Reid appreciated the nostalgia as he walked past the cafeteria. He had gotten into his fair share of mischief in high school. The senior prank of painting the mascot rainbow colors was still one of his favorite days of school. The harmless prank had resulted in detention for the boys, where they spent many hours touching up paint on the murals around the school. Hopefully Millie didn't know about his reputation for trouble as a student.

He was so lost in thought, he almost knocked Derek over when the kids stopped in front of the classroom door.

"We're here," Derek said.

"Want us to come in with you?" Madison hid her phone behind her back. "For moral support, of course."

Bree began to laugh. "Let's leave him alone. It will be more embarrassing if he doesn't have anyone else to help shield the buckle."

"You do know I live with you, right?" Reid straightened

his collar. "Don't be surprised if you find a frog in your bed one of these days."

"That's our cue to leave," Bree said. She gave her brother a hug. "You've got this. Miss Millie seems pretty cool."

"Thanks, Bree. I'll see you at home." Reid waited until the students had turned the corner before he knocked on the door. He wasn't sure what the proper protocol for picking up a teacher at school was, but he was fairly certain it didn't involve barging into her classroom.

Millie's eyes widened slightly when she opened the door, but then she waved him in. "Thanks for picking me up," she said.

Reid waited for the inevitable comment about the belt buckle to come out, but Millie seemed oblivious to it. That was a new one for him. Every other date he had been on had started with some sort of comment about the buckle, whether it was a compliment, a criticism, or outright laughter. The rule was that you had to wear the belt until the woman had reacted. Then you could take it off.

Reid glanced around the classroom while Millie grabbed her purse. The teacher was clearly a minimalist. She had a few posters with grammar rules hanging from the walls, but most of the room was bare. The only messy thing in the room was a giant whiteboard filled with what looked like character types. He walked closer to start reading the list.

"Your best friend's fiancé's brother?" he asked, feeling a little self-conscious. "What is this list for?"

Millie's cheeks pinked up. "We were making a list of

possible side characters for a book. You may have come up."

"I'm a side character now? Do you really think I'm that ridiculous?" Reid jutted out his hip, giving Millie the perfect opening to comment on the belt buckle but she reached for her sweater.

"I didn't say that was a bad thing. A side character is someone who adds personality to the story."

"True." Reid winked at Millie. "I'll do my best to give you something to tell your students about tomorrow."

"Should I be worried?" Although she was a head shorter than him, Reid could feel the weight of her stare.

"Not at all." Reid held his arm out, and together they left the school. He saw a flash out of the corner of his eye seconds before he heard his sister's giggle. This date was definitely going to be on social media. Hopefully Millie had a thick skin.

* * *

REID WAS DIPPING his fries in fry sauce when Millie finally commented on the belt buckle. The date had been going well enough, so far. They had more in common than Reid had expected. If he wasn't careful, he was going to be tempted to ask her out again.

They had been talking about the work Reid did at the ranch. He was explaining about how they would plant the fields when Millie began laughing.

"What did I miss?" He raised an eyebrow, trying to figure out what would be funny about a crop of hay.

Millie glanced at her watch. "I have a confession to make. Hazel told me you'd probably show up wearing that ridiculous belt buckle. I didn't think she was right. We may have made a bet about it."

Reid pushed the fries to the side. "A bet about the belt?"

"Yeah. I told Hazel there was no way you'd make it into the restaurant with the thing on, but she said you would wear it until I said something." She was wiping tears of laughter from her eyes. "I didn't think Hazel could possibly be right, but she was."

"You made me keep it on for a bet?" Reid tried to scowl, but he started cracking up. "That's a first for me." He took the belt off, hanging it over the side of the chair beside him. It felt so much easier to breathe without the buckle jabbing into his stomach every time he moved.

"I figured as much. According to Hazel, you guys have all taken turns wearing it." Millie's smile dropped. "It sounds like you've worn it the most though."

And there it was. The reason why Reid was trying to make a good impression on Millie. He wasn't interested in settling down and getting married, but that didn't make him a bad guy. Was it really a problem that he wasn't ready to commit to anyone yet?

It was time to shift the attention elsewhere. "I've been on my fair share of dates. Some of them have been disastrous. What about you? Do you have any crazy dating stories?"

Millie pursed her lips together as if trying to hold back a smile. Finally, her mouth twitched, and she broke into a grin.

"I can't tell you how many people have tried to set me up over the years. There's something about being a teacher that makes people assume I'm lonely. I used to accept blind dates, but quickly learned that that was a mistake."

A flicker of envy shot through Reid, which he quickly tamped down. It didn't matter how many men Millie dated. "What's the worst date you've ever been on?"

Millie tucked her hair behind her ears. "It's a toss-up between muscles and the puker."

The nicknames alone piqued Reid's interest. "Tell me more."

"Muscles picked me up wearing black spandex shorts and a tight gold shirt."

"So, he had no fashion sense?" Most of the guys Reid knew didn't care much about what they wore, but this outfit sounded a bit extreme.

"It gets worse. He took me to a wrestling match. Part way through the date, he jumped up and climbed into the ring." Millie clasped her hands in front of her. "I thought he was joking, but nope. He was actually one of the competitors."

Reid snorted. "That's kind of hilarious."

"Not so much. By the time the wrestling matches were over for the night, I had a splitting headache. The guy kept dragging me from one side of the room to the other so he could introduce me as his girlfriend."

"I'm sorry." Reid couldn't stop laughing. "That sounds like the stuff they make up for movies."

"Yeah. I was never so happy to get home. The guy was harmless enough, but definitely not my type."

"So, I guess I should cancel my wrestling match for later this evening?" Reid raised his eyebrow, trying to look serious.

Millie shook her finger. "I've learned my lesson. Now I've got an escape plan if a date goes wrong."

That was an interesting piece of news to file away. Reid wondered how often Millie backed out of dates. So far, she seemed to be happy enough with him, but that could change at any time.

"Tell me about pukey."

Millie's laughter stopped. "That one was more sad than anything. The guy was so nervous, he didn't make it through dinner. They were bringing out our main dishes when he began to vomit. Let's just say that I had to throw away a good pair of shoes that were ruined that night."

"Poor guy. Did you find out what was up?"

"He says it was food poisoning, but I'll admit, I didn't really give him a second chance. There are some things you can't come back from."

"True. I'm sure the guy was mortified."

Reid was impressed with Millie's good sense of humor. Both experiences sounded awful, for different reasons. He was reaching for his glass of water when he was tackled from the side in a big hug. The momentum pushed him forward enough to send the cup flying across the table. It spun once before landing on Millie's side with a clank.

Her eyes widened as the water splashed across her food and continued its path down the front of her dress. The hubbub in the diner stilled as all eyes turned to them.

Reid tried to reach for the napkins, but his arms

couldn't move. He turned his head, knowing in his gut that he wasn't going to like what he saw.

"I thought I'd find you here, silly. I was going to ask you on another date, but then you came to our special spot."

Lydia. Of all the people to find Reid on a date, why did it have to be the one woman who couldn't take no for an answer? Reid was at a loss for words. How was he supposed to help Millie if he couldn't get Lydia to leave?

Millie answered the question for him when she stood, her dress dripping with water. Her expression wasn't hard to read when she asked a nearby employee for the closest bathroom. Reid was in trouble again, but this time he hadn't done anything to cause it.

He watched Millie storm off. He hadn't expected to care about the teacher, but the thought that she was angry with him stabbed him to the core. He had been trying so hard to have a good reputation.

Growling softly, Reid turned to Lydia. "I am only going to say this once. We are not dating. We will never be dating. Please leave."

The words were harsh, but Lydia didn't seem to respond to subtle hints. Instead of leaving, she pulled up a dry chair and plopped down at the table, burying her face in her hands as she loudly began to cry.

"Why won't you admit your feelings for me? I know you felt the same connection I did when we met. When are you going to let me in?"

Lydia lifted her face from her hands. Dark trails of mascara ran from her eyes. It would be comical if she wasn't drawing the attention of every person in the diner.

Reid wanted to sink into the ground to avoid the eyes staring at him.

"I never said I have feelings for you. We've only been on one date."

"So, you chose to date that pixie of a school teacher instead? What does she have that I don't?"

A number of unkind words raced through Reid's mind, but he wasn't going to stoop to her level.

"I'm sorry you misunderstood our relationship." The words sounded odd coming off his tongue. They didn't have a relationship. They didn't even have a friendship. "I really do mean it when I say that I am not interested in you."

That brought out a new set of wails, although Reid could see that there were no tears in her eyes. Was Lydia really that desperate for him or had someone put her up to the whole thing? In the end it didn't matter. He was sitting at a table with a woman he couldn't stand while the woman he was interested in was stuck in a bathroom trying to salvage her outfit.

In a matter of minutes, he had managed to make not one, but two women mad at him. That was a new record.

Reid cleared his throat. "That's all there is to see, folks. Thanks for coming to the show." He grabbed his phone and the belt and headed to the front of the diner to pay. Even if Millie came out of the bathroom to give him another chance, the date was over.

Intelligent, beautiful women like Millie didn't put up with drama. Reid's one chance to smooth things over with Millie before the wedding was ruined before it even began.

CHAPTER 6

Millie hadn't stuck around long enough to identify the busty redhead who had flung herself at Reid. All she knew was that the woman was obviously comfortable around Reid, and that this date was officially over.

Her dress was soaked, but at least it was only water and not sticky soda. Millie dabbed at her dress, trying to soak up as much water as she could. She was going through a lot of paper towels, but what choice did she have? It wasn't like she'd brought an extra change of clothes with her.

Her breath hitched in her throat the first few times the bathroom door opened. Was Reid going to march in and check on her in the women's room? As the minutes went by, Millie realized that him not checking on her was much worse. It meant that he had gone home with the redhead, and she was going to have to call someone for a ride.

The only friend Millie wasn't furious with was Sheila,

but they weren't close. They were school buddies. Not bail your friend out of a jam buddies.

Millie knew she should call Hazel, Dawn, or Steph, but she was too irritated with them. It was their fault she was on the date in the first place. They were the ones who pushed Reid and Millie together because they didn't want to be stuck with the guy. Her phone was sitting on the table anyway so figuring out who to call was pointless.

The door swung open again and a waitress poked her head inside. "I saw what happened, hun. You okay?"

"Yeah. I'm just going to dry off a bit more if that's okay."

The waitress nodded. "You take all the time you need."

There was something in her tone that made Millie look up. "She's still out there, isn't she?"

Everyone in the diner had been watching. The waitress would know exactly who she was referring to.

"Sorry, hun. She looks pretty upset." She leaned in close and began to whisper. "I know it's none of my business, but is she the other woman, or are you?"

Millie covered her mouth to hold in the laughter. "Oh, believe me. I'm not one of his girls in any way, shape, or form. As far as I'm concerned, that woman out there is who he deserves."

"That's the spirit." The waitress patted her arm. "I'll leave you to it."

She walked out, leaving Millie behind with swirling thoughts. She was furious with Reid, but did she have a right to be? All the guy had done was spill some water on her, and that most definitely had been an accident.

Millie taught about parables and fables every year in

her classroom. Each story helped teach a lesson. How many times had she told her students the story of the man who helped a snake, and in return, got bitten? The man knew the snake was dangerous, but he ignored his better judgment and got hurt.

Was Reid really any different? He had a reputation for dating lots of women. Why should she be surprised that he turned on the charm with her? He had an impish smile and he was easy to talk to. It wasn't any stretch to realize that he had a fan club.

Millie's skirt wasn't dry, but the water was no longer dripping from it. She patted it down with a paper towel for a final time and then took a deep breath. It was time to retrieve her purse from the table no matter how many people were watching. She was more than ready to go home and change into something more comfortable.

A quick glance through a crack in the door showed that the coast was clear. Thankfully, the redhead was gone. So was Reid.

Millie pushed back a flash of annoyance. She hadn't expected him to stick around, but she hoped he'd be enough of a gentleman to make sure her stuff was okay. So much for making assumptions.

The helpful waitress from the bathroom was wiping down the table. She looked up when Millie approached. "I'm afraid your food is a goner. Do you want me to make you a new plate on the house?"

Sticking around to wait for food in a diner full of people who had seen her humiliation sounded awful. "No, but thanks for the offer. I'm ready to head home." Millie reached for her purse, throwing the strap over her shoulder.

"I'll see you next time," the waitress said, patting her arm.

Millie was almost to the door when Reid's voice rang out. "Hey. Wait for me."

She sped up, pretending like she didn't hear him. The guy had some nerve, thinking she'd want to talk to him. The door was swinging shut when Reid caught it.

"Will you please stop so we can talk?" The belt buckle was dangling from his arm, a reminder that they hadn't exactly started off the date in a normal way. Was it really any surprise that it was ending crazily as well?

Millie walked to the bench outside and sat down, gasping as her legs pressed against the cold metal. She hadn't dressed for spending much time outside. As much as she wanted to make a dramatic exit, she still didn't have a ride home. She wasn't about to lead Reid on a foot chase across the parking lot. That would make her look even more ridiculous.

"What do you want, Reid?" Millie crossed her arms in front of her chest.

He blinked slowly, his eyes wide with concern. "I want to make sure you're okay."

The way Reid was looking at her made her understand why women fawned all over him. He had mastered his sincere, look straight into your soul, face, but she knew it was an act.

"I'll be better once this date is over and I'm home."

Reid gave a small nod. "I expected as much. Can I explain?"

Millie wanted to say no, but she was stuck. "Make it quick."

"That was Lydia."

So, the redhead had a name. Millie didn't care. "Knowing her name doesn't exactly help."

"Her brother Gideon is catering the weddings. I agreed to go out with Lydia as a favor to him, but I had no idea how possessive she could be." Reid rubbed the back of his neck, giving her a half-smile.

Millie had expected a whiny answer about some ex-girlfriend. She didn't know how to respond to a set-up.

Reid searched her eyes, but she didn't answer. He held his hands out, palms up. "Look. I know how people gossip about me. I'm sure you've heard a few unflattering things."

Millie nodded. "Maybe a few."

Reid leaned forward. "Have you ever heard me called a liar?"

He had a point. "No, but there's always a first time for everything."

"I'm asking you to believe me. Try to see it from my side and not from the side of a crazy woman who is borderline stalking me."

Reid's explanation sounded plausible, but Millie wasn't ready to let him off the hook. "How do I know you're not the one stalking her? Maybe you were just using this little date to make her jealous." She folded her arms across her chest to keep from shivering. "Do you have a problem with letting go?"

It was fun teasing Reid. His face turned red, but then his eyes lit up.

"I've got a little proof." He held out his phone, swiping until he got to the text messages. "Start here."

As Millie scrolled through the dozens of unanswered texts, she could see what Reid was talking about. She looked at him, raising her eyebrows as the list kept going.

Reid grimaced. "That doesn't include the voicemails."

"How long has she been like this?" Millie handed the phone back. As much as she hated to admit it, Reid was looking innocent.

"Would you believe me if I told you she got my number last week? It feels like it's been months. I'd like to never speak to her again, but he's the caterer."

The pieces were fitting together. "And you don't want anything to mess up the weddings."

"Yeah." Reid slipped out of his jacket and held it out to Millie. "Here. You've got to be freezing. If you want to end our date, I totally understand."

Millie slipped her arms into the sleeves and hugged the jacket close. The jacket smelled strongly of Reid's cologne.

"Are you okay driving me home? I'd rather not walk back into that restaurant."

Reid nodded. "Of course."

The drive home started out silent, but then Reid began to chuckle. "I think you made a friend back there."

"What do you mean?" There hadn't been anyone else around.

"The waitress was ready to throw me through the meat grinder. I barely got my belt back from her."

Millie's heart warmed at the thought of a stranger watching out for her. "I'll have to thank her next time I go in."

Reid glanced at Millie before he turned back to the road. "Can I be honest with you?"

"I'd hope so."

"I asked you out on this date because I wanted to smooth things over with you. We kind of started off on the wrong foot." His forehead was creased while he gripped the steering wheel.

"I already forgave you for the parking spot." Millie wanted to pat his shoulder, but that felt a little too intimate in the closed space. "I guess you're right. We didn't start off so well. Why do you care what I think?"

Reid rubbed his chin. "I don't know if I can explain it. The past number of years have been tough on my family. I mean, we've worked hard, and the ranch is doing well, but our personal lives have been a bit of a mess."

Millie bit the side of her cheek to keep from commenting. It seemed like Reid had done plenty well enough for himself.

"Now that my brothers are finally getting ready to settle down, I feel like all the pressure is turning to me. When am I going to get married? When am I going to start a family?"

"That isn't fair of them to expect that from you." Millie felt a pang of sadness for Reid. She had seen too many friends buckle under family pressures.

"They don't say it directly, but it is an unspoken current that is there no matter what I do. I guess I thought that if you and I were friends, it would take the pressure off me, at least for this wedding."

The corner of Reid's mouth lifted. "Although I think I've bombed it with you more spectacularly than I ever have with the woman I was actually trying to impress."

"You weren't trying to impress me?" Millie started to laugh. "I mean, you did wear that gorgeous belt buckle."

Reid shook his head. "I haven't dated a lot of women in the past."

Millie smacked his shoulder. "I thought we were being honest. You've got quite the track record, Mister."

"Let me rephrase that. I haven't had a serious relationship for years. I keep things light and commitment free so no one gets hurt. That's why I started off wearing that silly belt."

Millie thought back to the comments from her friends. "You don't really know how women think, do you?"

"Why do you say that?"

"Let's just say that I've talked to a few of the women you've ditched. There may have been some hurt feelings." Millie ran her fingers along the edge of her seatbelt.

"Huh." Reid pulled into her driveway, putting the car in park. "Why didn't they say anything?"

Millie shook her head. "I'm pretty sure they thought you wouldn't care. When a guy ghosts a woman after taking her out, that's a pretty clear rejection."

Reid turned his full gaze on Millie. "Even after just one date?"

"Yes. Even after one date. Did you really think they wouldn't notice?" Millie was used to helping students work through their problems. It really wasn't her business who Reid dated in the future, but if she could help him look at things from a different angle, maybe she could help prevent a few broken hearts.

The silence filling the car was heavy. Millie knew that sometimes questions took a minute to answer.

"I hoped they wouldn't. Now I feel like the world's biggest jerk." Reid rubbed his hands along his jeans. "I didn't know that was my reputation. How do I fix it?"

Millie was surprised at the question. She expected Reid to be more defensive. "Your reputation? The way I see it, there are two ways to get out of it."

"Lay it on me." Reid flexed his fingers.

"You need to either start dating someone for real, or you need to stop dating all together." She didn't think Reid was capable of either situation.

He was silent for a moment before he turned in his seat to face her. "What if there's a third way?" A smile broke across Reid's face, lighting his eyes.

"Like what?"

Reid leaned towards Millie. "What if I started to fake date someone? Just until the weddings are over. That would get everyone off my back."

The conversation was veering wildly off track. Millie needed to reign him back in. "You'd have to find someone willing to go along with the ruse. Someone who was immune to your charms."

Reid smirked. "Someone who was willing to give it to me straight, even when I messed up?"

The sides of the car were closing in on Millie, but

she ignored the warning bells. "Yeah. It would have to be someone who knew the plan, and who was willing to go through with it. No falling in love. No real emotions."

"Do you think it could work? Could a fake relationship really get my family off my back?" Reid's eyes lit up like someone was handing him a million dollars.

"I don't know your family well, but I'm guessing yes. They'll be so busy dealing with weddings, they won't pay much attention to your relationship."

The energy in the air was electric. Millie watched Reid, his face lighting up with hope. Stripped of his bad boy reputation, Reid was just a regular guy who was trying to make things better for himself and his family. There was nothing wrong with wanting to keep the focus on his brothers who were in the spotlight.

As fast as the light had come, the happiness in Reid's eyes faded. "One problem. I don't know a single woman who would agree to this."

Millie swallowed hard, trying to stop the words from leaving her mouth. "What about me?"

"That isn't funny." Reid's fingers drummed against the steering wheel.

"I'm being serious." Millie had to choose her words wisely. "I told you about everyone trying to set me up. Maybe, if I had a fake boyfriend, they'd leave me alone for a while, too."

"That's a big ask."

Reid was saying the right words, but Millie could see the hope in his eyes. "I'm a big girl. I know what my heart can and can't handle. Right now, getting a break from the dating world sounds amazing."

"Are we really going to do this?" Reid held his hand out for Millie.

She grabbed his hand and pumped it up and down. "We already know we've got to hang out for Thomas and Hazel's wedding. Why not give it a try?"

Reid whooped and pulled Millie in for a hug. Her heart was beating fast when she pulled back.

"If we're going to do this, we need some rules." Millie wasn't about to start a fake relationship without some ground rules in place.

Reid yawned, quickly covering his mouth. "I agree. Can we make them tomorrow? The way I see it, I owe you another dinner. Any chance we can go on a second date?"

The time for caution had passed. Millie was in, but she wasn't going to make it easy for Reid. "I don't know. I'm not a fan of getting doused with water."

"I promise next time things will go better."

Millie's heart was thumping, making her glad she was the only one who could hear it. "You can't promise that."

Reid reached for her hand, gently hooking his pinky finger around hers. "I pinky promise that if you give me a chance, our next date will go better. And in my family? That promise is more binding than any contract."

There was nothing that gave Millie any reason to trust Reid other than his word, but the flutters of excitement dancing through her body was all the confirmation she needed. She was ready for an adventure.

"Until next time, cowboy."

Millie climbed out of the mustang and headed into the house. She pulled the curtain back from the window and watched Reid drive away, her heart slowly returning to a steady beat. If she wasn't careful, she was going to fall for the guy just like all the women did in the romance novels she read.

She sternly reminded herself that this relationship was nothing more than a tool to get men off her back. Shrugging out of Reid's jacket, she gave herself another stern shake. His jacket wasn't any different than her own jacket, even if the cologne that lingered on it smelled like grass and cedar with a bit of sage.

Fake dating Reid was going to be much harder than she thought. They needed some rules, fast, before her heart got involved.

What had she just agreed to do?

CHAPTER 7

$\mathcal{R}$eid couldn't believe his luck. He was standing at the kitchen counter, holding a folded white piece of paper between his hands. Bree had delivered the answer to his second note when she got home from school, tossing it on the counter with a smile.

"I can't believe you and the teacher are passing notes back and forth like kids." Bree poured herself a glass of orange juice. "What is this one about?"

"Nothing much. She's probably just confirming our date tonight."

As expected, Bree pumped her fist in the air. "Yes. So that means things went well last night?"

"They did." Reid tapped his boot on the floor, not wanting to seem too eager to open the note. He waited until Bree left the room before he pounced.

Same time, same place? Come prepared with your demands.

Reid was beginning to recognize Millie's dry humor.

She was right though. What did Reid really want from a fake relationship? That was new territory for him.

He went back to the fields, glad that he had been inside when Bree got home. The note was cryptic, but Reid didn't want to explain to his siblings what was going on. The point of a fake relationship was to have people believe it.

By the time Reid was pulling into the Cluck's parking lot, his knee couldn't stop bouncing. He was a jumble of nerves. Reid recognized the feeling. This is why he usually stopped talking to a woman after the first date. Second dates came with more expectations.

He parked at the back of the lot so he'd have a longer walk to clear his mind. This wasn't a real date. This was nothing more than a planning session. People participated in planning sessions all over the world. All Reid had to do was pretend like he was heading into a business meeting.

The cafe was busy enough that Reid couldn't spot Millie. Small booths lined the room, with old-time movie posters hanging on the walls near each table. A thin shelf ran the perimeter of the room, displaying a collection of vintage items. Reid's favorite were the old toy cars. He could imagine the hours children had spent playing with them over the years.

Reid was studying a rusty Ford Model T when he felt a sharp tap on the shoulder. It was the waitress from the night before.

"Can I help you with something?" There was a hint of hostility in her voice. She pressed her lips together in a thin line.

Reid tucked his hands in his pockets. "Have you seen

the woman I was here with last night? I was supposed to meet Millie at six, but I was running a little late." He glanced at the faces of a few more diners but Millie wasn't among them.

The waitress looked him up and down, straightening the black apron around her waist. "Which woman? The redhead or the pretty one with the dark hair?"

Her words were a reminder of the disaster that the previous night had been. "Millie was my actual date. The redhead was a surprise." He didn't know why he was bothering to explain this to the waitress. It really wasn't her business who Reid brought in. But then he remembered how protective she'd been of Millie.

The waitress shifted her position, planting her hands on her hips. "Did you ever think maybe you've been stood up? From what I saw last night, you probably deserve it."

That was a low blow. "We had a misunderstanding. That's why we're back here. I wanted Millie to get to taste your delicious food without it being soaked in water."

The waitress smirked. "I'll let the chef know she's got a fan." She glanced around the room and then at her watch. "I'll tell Millie you're here if I see her. She can decide if she wants to talk to you."

"Thanks." Reid walked to the waiting area at the front of the diner and sat on a wooden bench. According to his watch, Millie was only a few minutes later than he was.

He watched a small family leaving the diner. The kids all seemed happy enough, but the exhausted look on the parent's faces told a different story. That was just one more reason why Reid wasn't interested in seriously dating anyone. Relationships led to marriage and marriage often led to having a family. He wasn't interested in trying to raise a human when he was feeling so unsettled himself.

Reid looked up when the door opened. His heart dropped when he realized it wasn't his date. Maybe the waitress was right, and Millie wasn't really coming. The thought of being stood up rankled a bit. If Millie didn't want to meet, she could have texted him. It was possible that she was stuck in traffic though.

Instead of stressing, Reid leaned back against the wall and closed his eyes. One of his favorite country songs was playing on the radio.

The song was just getting to the chorus when Millie walked in.

"Hey, cowboy," she called. "What are you smiling about?"

"Seeing you?" Reid winked. He was trying to play it cool, but he was immensely relieved that she had shown up. The waitress had gotten into his head. "Are you ready for some nefarious plotting?"

Millie's cheeks lifted. "You know it. I'm ready to take over the town."

"Then let's get started." Reid waved down the hostess, who walked them to their table. This time, instead of being next to one of the picture windows in the front, Reid requested a more private table in the back. He was pretty sure there wouldn't be any repeat Lydia attacks, but it was good to be cautious.

They ordered appetizers. Millie waited until the waiter was gone before she pulled out a small notebook and a flowered pen. "I can't believe we are really doing this." She looked around the restaurant and then lowered her voice. "Are we really going to be fake dating? That's the stuff that happens in books and movies. Not real life."

Reid nodded. "I've thought about it all day. If we play it right, neither one of us will get hurt. Just think about how much easier our lives are going to be without people trying to set us up all the time."

"That's the main reason I'm doing this." Millie flipped through a few pages of the notebook to find an empty page. The tattered book was filled with writing.

Reid couldn't believe what he was seeing. "Are those all to-do lists?" The pages held dozens of checked items. "Or shopping lists?"

Millie held the notebook out. "They're my to-do lists. This is the fifth notebook I'm on."

"It sounds like you're committed, and way more organized than I could ever be." Reid knew people tried to keep lists all the time, but they usually ended up ignoring them.

"I had to be. My first year of teaching was a major disaster trying to keep up with everything. Between the lesson plans, cooking, cleaning, and budgeting, I felt like I was running on a hamster wheel." She took a sip of her water. "I set a goal to accomplish three tasks every day. They could be big or small, but as long as I finished them, I counted the day as a success."

"I can't imagine being able to work that way. My days are too chaotic." There wasn't exactly a time schedule to keep on the ranch. Reid knew when they'd feed the animals and a general planting schedule, but he always had to allow for something to go wrong. The best plowed field could be flooded if a freak rainstorm blew through. Or an animal could go into labor and need extra assistance in the middle of the night.

Millie held out the notebook. "Before you're too impressed, you should see the tasks for today." She pointed to the first item.

Reid began to laugh. "You really put meeting me on the list?"

"I have doing my laundry on there, too. And after dinner I'm going to head to the grocery store."

"I guess I feel flattered." Reid watched as Millie checked the box. "Hey. We haven't even made our plans yet."

"But I'm here with you. It counts."

Millie's mischievous smile was back. Reid clasped his hands and rested them on the table.

"So, how are we going to do this?"

Millie tapped the pen against the notebook. "I think we both are clear on our goals, right? We have to date long enough to convince everyone we are in a real relationship. Then, when people have stopped paying attention to us, we break up. Does that sound good?"

"Yep." Reid smiled as Millie began to write. "What are you writing? We haven't made any rules yet."

Millie held the paper out. "Rule one. No falling in love for real. It's the rule I've been thinking about all day. That is the best way to protect our hearts."

"I like it. What else?" Reid was interested to hear what Millie had to say.

"I thought we should figure out some sort of a dating

schedule. People aren't going to believe we're an item if we're never together."

Their waitress from the previous night walked up, her face an unreadable mask as she set a plate of loaded baked potato skins on the table. "Can I get you anything else?" The question was directed to Millie.

"We're good. Thanks."

Reid lowered his voice when she walked away. "Some people aren't going to believe we're together even if we do hang out. I don't think she likes me very much. She's not even our server tonight, but I think she wanted to check on you."

Millie smirked. "That's sweet, but she's not the person I'm worried about. It's your family, mainly."

That made a lot of sense. Reid knew his family would definitely have questions. "So, how about for the second rule we make sure to spend a lot of time with either your friends or my family? If they see us together, it will be easier to believe in the relationship."

"Got it. Rule two. No more super-secret planning dates. Hang out in public."

The list was off to a great start, but then Reid remembered how he usually acted around women he liked. "Uh, we're forgetting something. If we're hanging out together, there's going to have to be some, well, affection."

Millie's face flushed from the tips of her ears all the way down her neck. "I wasn't thinking about that part of it. I mean, I've watched enough rom com movies to know that they are going to expect us to kiss." She looked at him with wide eyes, holding her hand to her mouth in mock horror. "Are you doing this so you can kiss me?"

"Nope." The word flew out of Reid's mouth, taking Millie's teasing grin with it.

"Ouch. Would kissing me really be a bad thing?" She crossed her legs, one foot bouncing up and down.

A fake relationship wasn't going to last if Reid was already offending his woman. "It's not that I don't want to kiss you."

"So, you have thought about it." She was looking at him in a way that made his insides squirm.

The conversation was derailing quickly. It was time to get back on track. "Kissing is kind of the last step, right? What about some of the middle ones? Like, I could put my arm around you."

Millie laughed. "Can you do it with a fake yawn like we're thirteen and sitting next to each other for the first time?"

Reid shook his head. "You're nuts, but yes, I can do that."

"What about holding hands?"

Reid fiddled with his shirt collar. Was the room getting warmer? "Are you talking attached at the hip, can't be away from each other for more than thirty seconds, hand holding?"

"Definitely not." Millie bit the side of her cheek. "I thought you were touchy-feely with all your dates."

"I used to be. You saw how Lydia acted, and that was after just a simple dinner date. I tend to attract women who get clingy. One minute we're holding hands, the next, she's proposing."

"Got it. Rule three. Only show as much affection as we have to in order to sell the relationship."

Reid groaned. "You're putting a rule that minimizes how much physical interaction we have?"

"I'm saying our public displays can be minimal. I've met plenty of couples who keep their affection to themselves."

Reid nodded. "Agreed. Minimal PDA." He wanted to believe Millie's words, but he had been burned too many times. The thought of holding Millie's hand was making him sweat. He could keep the lines between real and fake relationships separate, but could she? Or was he inviting yet another woman to believe she was Reid's entire world?

Millie seemed to sense his discomfort. "Rule four. No getting attached."

"Isn't that a given?" Reid took a bite of his food, trying to keep his face straight. She was reading his mind.

"Yes, but it is also my promise to you that I won't get clingy. You can put your arm around me or hold my hand and I promise I won't read anything into it."

Reid's breathing was slowing down. He didn't have any reason to trust Millie, but she sounded sincere. "Same here. What about pet names? Do you want me to call you honey or cupcake or something?"

Millie started laughing. "I'm not picky. If something comes up, let's go with it. Otherwise, no pressure."

That was easy enough. Reid passed the plate of potato skins to Millie. They had been sharing the appetizers back and forth. "Do you want the last one?"

"How about we split it? So, anything else for the list?"

Reid wiped his mouth with a napkin and set it back down in his lap. "What about dates? I know we're going to Thomas and Hazel's wedding together. Are there any places you want me to go with you?"

Millie groaned. "I forgot about the PTA bake sale this weekend. Do you want to help me man a booth for a couple of hours on Saturday?"

"As long as I get a cupcake for my efforts."

Millie wrote a new section in the notebook and under-lined the words "Date Ideas". She wrote down the wedding and the bake sale. "Anything else?"

"How do you feel about Sunday dinners? All the siblings will be back in another month. Can you handle dinner with my very chaotic family?" It was a big ask.

Millie wrote it in the notebook. "Dinner with your family sounds like a basic step." She dropped the pen, her eyes opening wide. "Hazel goes to family dinner, right? And Emily?"

"Yep."

"Well, I hope you're really serious about this because as soon as Hazel sees us together, she's going to tell our friends."

The greasy potato skins weren't settling well in Reid's stomach. He was tempted to call the entire thing off. It would be easy to shut the idea down and chalk it up to a momentary lapse of judgment. But then Reid remem-bered what he was going to get out of the ruse. Some good-natured ribbing from his brothers was worth the stress if he didn't have people setting him up left and right.

He lifted his eyes to Millie's, searching them to see if she was sincere. "I'm ready to do this if you are."

Millie didn't blink. She looked back at Reid, her eyes radiating determination. Then she grabbed the notebook. "One more thing."

She wrote the last rule and then signed her name.

Reid smiled when he took the notebook. "Rule five. We promise to have fun." He signed his name alongside hers. "I like it. Let the games begin."

* * *

THE REST of the meal flew by. When they left the restaurant, Reid knew all sorts of details about Emily, from why she decided to be a teacher to how old she was when she had her first kiss. Fake dating her was going to be a piece of cake.

Reid made sure to close the front door loudly when he got home. He made his way to the kitchen proudly carrying his container of leftovers. Sure enough, it didn't take long for Thomas to wander into the room.

"Where did you go?" Thomas asked.

"On my date?" Reid knew the drill. Short, sweet sentences would make Thomas curious.

"Yeah. Did you have fun?"

Reid shrugged. "It was just a first date. We went to Clucks."

Thomas leaned against the counter. "Anyone I know?"

Reid gulped. Was he ready to start the gossip chain going? The second he said Millie's name, Hazel would hear about it. Thomas couldn't keep a secret from his fiancé, and Reid wouldn't ask him to.

He set the food on the counter and pulled out his phone when it dinged.

Thanks for dinner.

Millie's text made him smile. She was the politest person he'd ever fake dated.

Reid typed a quick reply. **Did you make it home okay?**

Yep. I'm sitting on the couch with Rex.

Reid could imagine Millie; her body smothered by the large dog. **You're already hanging out with another guy?**

Yeah, but he drools a lot more than you do.

Reid couldn't help but laugh. He stuffed his phone back in his pocket and looked at Thomas. "Anything exciting happening here?"

Thomas crossed his arms. "Nice try. I think you were about to tell me who you were out with."

Reid placed the container of leftovers in the fridge and shut the door, his mind made up. He wanted Millie to be the first one to spill the beans. "I'll tell you if anything comes of it."

He tried to suppress a grin as he headed up to his room. The first step in getting his family to believe he was dating someone was to make sure he told them as little as possible. They were used to hearing his stories about the clingy women he had been out with. The more he kept from them, the more curious they'd be.

There was another ding as Reid was heading into his room. He flopped down on his bed and pulled out his phone. There was a new message from Millie. It was a selfie with her and the large boxer.

Rex says hi. How do you feel about a play date at the park one day?

Reid had been right in his assessment. Rex's head looked as big as Millie's. **That sounds great. Give him a tummy rub from me.**

Will do. Goodnight, cowboy.

Goodnight, teacher.

As Reid got ready for bed, he couldn't stop smiling. Millie was definitely following the last rule. Keep it fun. Hopefully they'd be able to be convincing as a couple together. His future sanity depended on it.

CHAPTER 8

The smell of fresh baked cupcakes permeated the air. Millie had come home from work and gotten started on her donation for the school fundraiser. She was measuring powdered sugar into a bowl when her phone began to ring.

"Just a second," she called out, even though the phone couldn't hear her.

Rex lifted his head and cocked his ears back. Then he settled back down for his nap.

After quickly wiping her hands on a dish towel, Millie was ready. She answered the phone on the last ring.

"Hey Reid. What's up?" It had been three days since they made their dating rules, but Millie had been talking to Reid every day. People weren't going to believe they were dating if she knew nothing about the guy.

"I'm checking in to make sure we're set for our date tomorrow." Reid's voice was low and raspy. Reid had seemed perfectly healthy when they went to dinner, but now he was sounding pretty bad.

Millie leaned back against the counter, her stomach sinking. This was going to be their first trial run of fake dating. She couldn't ask him to go if he was sick. "Are you feeling okay?"

"I had to yell to be heard over a lot of tractors today. My voice should be back to normal by tomorrow. What time should I pick you up?"

A little jolt of happiness zinged through Millie. They were really going to do this. Part of her couldn't believe that she was going to parade Reid Matthews around the school as her boyfriend. They were going to attract a lot of attention.

She had been hoping for a trial run, of sorts, to let her practice sitting close to Reid. He was going to attract attention in public, so they needed the relationship to look genuine. She couldn't jump or look startled if he reached for her hand. Unfortunately, his schedule had been too busy to squeeze in a practice date.

"We need to be there around 9:30 to help with any last-minute setup problems. Are you okay if I drive though? I've got way too many cupcakes sitting on my counter right now. I want to load them before Rex gets any snack ideas."

Reid's strained laugh came through the phone. "Smart. I'll be ready to go by 9:15."

Millie gulped. "Are we really doing this?"

"The bake sale? I thought so."

"No. Are you sure we're ready to go public? What if we

can't pass as boyfriend and girlfriend?" Millie was already imagining the teasing she'd get from her students.

Reid cleared his throat. "I am ready if you are. It could fail spectacularly, but then we'd have a story for Thomas and Hazel's wedding. What do you think?"

Millie closed her eyes. "I think I have far too many cupcakes to decorate right now. I'll stress about that and try to relax about our date. It's going to be fine."

"There you go. We've got this." Reid hung up the phone and Millie got back to work. She had purchased all the supplies to make ladybug cupcakes. It would have been so much easier to go with a simple frosting, but Millie wanted this to be the biggest fundraiser of the year. Cute cupcakes always sold out first.

She was adding red food coloring to a second batch of frosting when there was a knock at the door. Millie pulled the curtain to the side to see Reid standing on the steps, his hands tucked in his pockets.

Her heart fluttered when she pulled open the door. "Hi Reid. What are you doing here?"

"If you were my real girlfriend, I wouldn't want you to have to do a huge project on your own." He shrugged. "It sounded like you could use a hand so put me to work."

Millie opened the door wide and stepped to the side so Reid could come in. "You might be frightened when you see the kitchen."

Reid laughed. "I grew up in a family with eight kids. I'm not afraid of any messes."

He stopped talking when they turned the corner. Every surface of Millie's kitchen was covered with cupcakes and baking supplies. The kitchen sink overflowed with cupcake tins, mixing bowls, and spatulas. There was even a section of the wall that was covered in splotches of red frosting from the beaters.

Reid lifted one of the spatulas. "Are you making cupcakes or planning a massacre?"

Millie put her hands on her hips. "I warned you it wasn't going to be pretty." She went to the corner of the counter where a dozen finished ladybugs sat. "Look how cute they are when they are done, though."

"My sisters would love these." Reid scanned the kitchen. "So, where do you want me to start? The dishes, maybe?"

It was sweet of him to offer, but the dishes could sit overnight if they had to. The priority was getting the cupcakes decorated.

"How good are you with a knife?"

Reid chuckled. "I'd like to say proficient, but now you've got me worried. What do you need me to do?"

"You can either cut the chocolate cookies in half for the wings or you can spread frosting on the cupcakes." Millie reached for a cutting board.

"I'm guessing it's easier to cut cookies in half. Won't they stand out against the red?"

"I'm covering the cookies with a thin layer of red frosting, so the ladybug looks like it's spreading its wings to fly."

"And then you add the black dots?"

"Yep. And the face."

Reid rubbed his chin. "You said you're trying to do how many of these?"

"Hey. No judging." Millie elbowed him in the ribs. "Are you here to criticize or help?"

"Sorry." Reid took the small knife that Millie handed him. "I'm definitely here to help."

Millie slid a stack of small cookies across the counter to him. "I'll frost the bottom layer and pass the cupcakes to you. You can cut the cookies in half and fan them out on top of each cupcake. Then I'll finish them off."

"That sounds ominous." Reid's eyes twinkled when he was joking.

Millie shook her head. This wasn't the time to be getting distracted by the handsome man standing in her kitchen.

Reid cut the first cookie in half. He spent a minute trying to place the wings in the exact right place before he settled on a position and passed it over for inspection. "Is this okay?"

The look of concentration on his face was adorable. Millie bumped him with her hip. "Relax. These cupcakes are for a bunch of high school students. They won't judge too much if the wings are slightly askew."

Reid began to laugh as he pointed to the five cupcakes Millie had already frosted and passed over to him in the time it took him to deliberate. "Alright, alright. I'll speed it up."

It didn't take long to sink into a rhythm. Millie's stress levels went down as the counter began to fill with little ladybugs. She had worried that working with Reid would be awkward, but the conversation flowed. Millie was laughing at one of Reid's stupid jokes when he raised his hand to her face, trailing his finger down her cheek.

Her breath hitched in her throat. It was a simple gesture, but his hand sent trails of heat that rushed to the spot where it rested.

"You had a blob of frosting on your cheek. Red might be your color, but I don't think frosting is the best way to wear it."

He was laughing about the encounter, like brushing frosting off someone's cheek was no big deal. This was why Millie needed a practice run. She couldn't deal with flutters in her stomach every time Reid reached for her.

"Thanks." Millie began to move the finished cupcakes onto platters, stepping away from Reid so the butterflies in her stomach could calm down. Rule number one. No falling in love for real. That would be so much easier to do if the cowboy wasn't such a gentleman.

It was getting late when they put the finishing touches on the cupcakes and loaded them into the back of Millie's car.

"Thanks for your help." Millie stood outside the door, expecting Reid to take off.

"Do you really think I'd skip out on the clean up?" Reid looked at Millie with soft eyes.

"I'd never ask someone else to take care of my mess for me." The butterflies were kicking up again. Millie needed them to calm down so she could sleep.

"And I'd never leave someone I care about with a kitchen that looks like it's one step away from being a crime scene." Reid leaned against the doorframe. "Besides, washing dishes is way easier than trying to clean a wedding veil." He winked at her. "How about I wash, and you dry? I'll let you put them away."

Millie took a quick breath of clean air. It was going to be much harder to keep her mind focused when she was back in the kitchen, breathing in his cologne.

"Let's do this." Millie headed back to the kitchen with Reid trailing behind. She looked at the mess and turned to him. "Thanks for coming to help me today. I think I'd be up for another couple of hours if you hadn't come along."

Reid stepped to the sink and turned the water on. "What kind of a friend would I be if I didn't help out?"

And there it was. The not-so-subtle reminder that Millie and Reid were nothing more than friends working on a project. Millie told the butterflies in her stomach to go back into hibernation before she got to work. There would be time for butterflies later when she found a real guy to date.

* * *

A GOOD NIGHT'S sleep helped Millie to find the proper perspective. She had a fundraiser to get to. She was planning out the way the booths would be set up when she pulled on to Old Ranch Road. She was mentally placing the paper plates and napkins when she pulled into Reid's driveway.

It wasn't until she was standing on his porch that she noticed Hazel's truck parked in front of the house. Millie's mouth went dry. The first test of their fake relationship was supposed to be in front of a crowd of acquaintances. Her co-workers weren't used to seeing her in love. They wouldn't be able to tell the difference between a fake smile and a real one.

Her best friend Hazel? That was a completely different story.

Millie was raising her hand to knock when Thomas flung the door open. "Hi Millie. We were expecting you." He turned and began to yell into the house. "He wasn't lying, guys. Millie is really here."

Millie's mouth dropped open. "Did you just make an announcement to your family? That's mortifying."

"Sorry, Millie. We're so used to teasing Reid, I didn't even think about it." Thomas led her to the family room, where Hazel was waiting to pounce.

"Reid told us that you were coming to pick him up, but I totally thought he was teasing. I'm pretty sure my best friend would have told me that she was dating my fiancé's brother."

Millie's stomach sank to her toes. "It's still pretty new." She was spared the agony of having to answer another question when Reid came into the room.

He walked over to her, the expression on his face difficult to read. Then he wrapped his arms around her, whispering in her ear. "Rule Two. Hang out in public. Just squeeze me back and we'll be on our way."

Reid was right. This is what they had wanted to happen. Millie hugged him tightly, reaching for his hand when they separated. "Are you ready to go?"

"Let's do this."

The smile on Millie's face was genuine when she followed Reid out of the house. He walked her to the driver's side of her car, opening the door for her. "They're still watching. Do you trust me?"

Millie nodded.

Reid leaned forward and rested his cheek next to hers. "From this angle, they'll think I'm giving you a kiss."

His breath was warm against her cheek. A wave of tingles flooded Millie's body. She lifted her hand to the back of his neck and gave it a little squeeze.

"This is going to be harder than I thought." Millie was finding it difficult to speak.

Reid straightened up. "No way. We just fooled my family and your best friend." He winked at her and walked around the front of the car to his door.

Millie barely had time to catch her breath before Reid folded himself into her car. His tall body filled the seat, but that wasn't why the air felt thick. Millie couldn't think straight. She wasn't an actress. How was she supposed to be a fake girlfriend? They weren't going to fool anyone.

She looked up when Reid reached for her hand. He gave it a gentle squeeze. "Relax. You did great. We made it through our first public appearance, and as far as I can tell, they bought it."

"What makes you say that?"

Reid jerked his head towards the house. "Because they're still watching us."

As Millie looked, she could see faces peeking out from behind the curtains. "They are ridiculous." She waved at Hazel as she backed out.

They were driving down Old Ranch Road when Millie let out a deep breath. "That was stressful."

"I know. Are you okay?" His words washed over Millie's heart.

She pulled on to the main road, heading towards the high school. "Yeah. I just wasn't expecting an audience."

"I guess it was a warmup for our day. Any last minute words?"

Millie laughed. "You live with a teenager so you know how they can be. I'd expect a little bit of teasing."

"I can handle it. Remember, I did show up to your school wearing a ridiculous gold belt buckle."

A quick glance in Reid's direction showed that he was completely relaxed. His arm rested against the middle console, but there was no nervous drumming of the fingers or jiggling of his knee. Millie felt a pang of jealousy.

So far, every time Reid had touched her, her body had responded. She wasn't quite sure how to handle having a handsome man put his cheek next to hers without feeling a little self-conscious. It wasn't like she was going to fall for the guy, but he was so much better at hiding his emotions than she was.

Millie wanted to say something, but she remembered rule four. No getting attached. If she started questioning Reid's casual attitude, she'd be crossing the line between a fake girlfriend and someone who was getting too close. It was better to keep things light.

Thankfully, they were almost to the school. They were pulling into the parking lot when Reid's knee began to bounce up and down.

"What's wrong?" Hazel turned off the engine.

"We forgot the most important thing. What if someone asks how we met?"

Millie smacked her forehead. "I can't believe we forgot that." She was racking her mind for a cute story before she realized what the answer would be.

"Reid, Bree is going to be at this fundraiser. She was there when we met at the dress shop."

"You're right." Reid's knee was still bouncing. "Is it a good enough story?"

It was Millie's turn for her nerves to kick in. "I guess in the end, it really doesn't matter what my friends think. I mean, it's the truth. I'd rather stick with the real story than try to embellish on a fake one."

"Good call." Reid pressed a hand down on his leg. "Alright. Let's do this."

He climbed out of the car and headed towards Millie's door. As he did, she said a quick prayer that they'd be able to pull the event off. It felt strange praying that the Lord would help her and Reid to be deceitful, but she was pretty sure He'd understand why they were doing it.

Reid opened the door and took her hand, helping her climb out of the car. They walked to the trunk, where he gave her hand a squeeze before letting go. "We've got this."

Millie popped the trunk and filled both of Reid's hands with cupcake trays. At least with their hands full, people wouldn't expect them to be cuddly.

They walked to the back of the school in a comfortable silence. Millie was on familiar grounds now. The school was like a second home to her. She'd be able to handle this event, fake boyfriend and all.

As they approached the back of the school, she was relieved to see that someone had thought ahead. The gym door was propped open. Millie and Reid were swarmed by teenagers when they entered. "We can take those trays," one of the students said. They took the trays from Millie and Reid's hands and ran off.

"Hi Miss G. You got anything else that needs to come in?" The young man standing in front of her wasn't someone she recognized.

"I do." She handed the keys to Reid. "Can you guys grab the rest of the cupcakes? I want to make sure everything is ready inside."

Reid nodded. "You've got it, babe."

The nickname rolled off Reid's tongue, but Millie cringed. Babe? That was one of her least favorite pet names. If they were going to be together for any amount of time, she was going to have to think of something better for him to call her.

A quick glance around the room told Millie the story she expected to see. Teachers and parents alike had been watching her exchange with Reid.

That was the moment she admitted to herself that she wanted this ruse to last for a while. They may be dating for the wrong reasons, but getting a school filled with matchmakers off her back? She could already feel the pressure lifting off her shoulders. Rule five. This was going to be fun.

CHAPTER 9

Watching Millie in her element was incredible. Reid had asked around a little bit to see if he could find out what sort of a teacher she was but seeing her interact with the students was surprising. No matter how chaotic the event got, Millie took the time to talk to each individual student that approached her.

They had started off the event together, but Reid soon separated from Millie's side. There were too many booths and, thanks to the cold that had been going around, not enough parents to man them. Reid offered to take charge of the doughnut booth, which was unfortunately on the other side of the room from Millie's cupcake booth.

So much for being seen together. The way things were going, no one would even remember that Reid and Millie had walked in at the same time. A few minutes after the event started, Reid noticed a tall, blonde-haired man who kept circling back to Millie's table. It didn't take a genius to figure out that the guy was interested in her.

Reid needed a plan, fast. He was trying to figure out what to do when one of the teens walked by with a handful of red heart-shaped balloons.

"Are those for sale?" Reid could feel the beginning of an idea forming.

The boy turned to face him. "Yep. $3 per balloon."

"Awesome. I'd like to buy them all." Reid pulled open his wallet.

"That's . . ." the kid trailed off so he could count the balloons. "There's fifteen of them here."

Reid nodded. "That's exactly how many I need." He handed over the money and got a handful of balloons in exchange. "Can you help me out with a favor?"

The kid nodded. He waited by the doughnut table while Reid tied all the balloons to a chair except for one. Reid grabbed a black marker and wrote R + M on the front and back in large letters.

Glancing up, Reid could see that the blonde-haired man was starting to approach Millie's table again. Reid handed the balloon to the teen. "Do you know Miss Grant?"

"Yeah. I have her for English."

"Awesome. Please take this to her and tell her it's from her boyfriend. I know you have other jobs to do so it's okay to jump to the front of the line."

The boy grinned and gave Reid a fist bump. "I'm on it."

Reid tried to look busy when the boy approached Millie's table. He watched as the boy cut in front of Blondie and handed the balloon over. Millie's face wrinkled with confusion. Then she saw the letters.

Reid was handing a doughnut to a customer when he

heard a sharp whistle. Millie was staring at him. "Thanks, cowboy," she called. She shook her head with an amused grin before turning her attention back to the next person in line.

Ten minutes later, the blonde guy was circling Millie's table again. Reid called over the first helper he could find. This time it was a teenage girl with a pin that read Team Captain.

"I'm guessing you're busy, but could you or one of your team members deliver this to Miss Grant for me? I can't leave my table." He held out a red balloon that he had drawn hearts all over.

The girl's face lit up. "You bet."

Reid had suspected that the teens were going to be great helpers, and he was right. He told her to cut to the front of the line and then got back to trying to sell donuts.

This time, he watched Millie's body shaking with laughter as the girl handed over the balloon. Millie met his eye and Reid winked. They weren't drawing a lot of atten-tion, but a few people were watching the interaction with interest, including Blondie. He got out of Millie's line and headed to the booth next door.

Unbelievably, the guy didn't get the hint. Five minutes later he was back in Millie's line. Reid saw Bree walking by with her friends Madison and Derek. "Hey, sis. Who is that guy over by Millie's table?"

"Mr. J?" Bree stood on her toes to see him better.

Derek nodded. "He's the tennis coach."

That complicated things a bit. If he was a colleague, there was a chance that Millie was fine talking to him. Reid wasn't sure. The guy looked more like someone trying to ask for a date than a teacher trying to discuss school. Reid could back off, but that wasn't part of their deal. Millie had said she was tired of people trying to set her up. He assumed that also meant she was tired of unwanted advances from the other teachers.

"Do you guys want to do me a favor?" Reid untied two more balloons and Bree began to bounce on her toes.

"Are you going to give those to Miss Millie?"

"Yep." He drew a flower on one balloon and a pair of ladybugs on the other with a heart above their heads. "Please tell Millie I miss her."

Madison took one balloon and Bree took the other. They were giggling as they walked over to the table. Derek looked back and gave Reid a thumbs up.

This time, Millie held her hands up in a heart shape. She blew a kiss to Reid, and then leaned over the table to whisper to Bree.

A few moments later, Bree was coming towards him, her hands behind her back. Her friends were walking on either side, shielding whatever she was carrying from Reid's sight. They stopped at a booth on the way, their heads close together while they discussed their options.

Reid had thought Millie was sending something back, but then Bree walked out of the room. The balloons did the trick though, because Mr. J finally turned his attention to a booth on Reid's side of the room.

He took a minute to study the man's face. The guy was slightly shorter than Reid, but he walked with confidence. He had thick blonde hair, which was something girls usually swooned over. Still, Reid wasn't sure what the appeal was.

Mr. J was making his way towards Reid's table, but trying to be nonchalant as he did so. Reid turned his attention back to restocking an empty plate. If the guy wanted to talk to him, he would. He was placing the new tray of donuts on the table when Bree came back.

She had a pen in one hand and a stack of papers in the other. She set the papers down on the table and then handed Reid a note.

His hands began to tremble as he opened it. Was he about to get in trouble for disrupting Millie's line? Maybe he should have told the kids to wait their turn. He read Millie's words and began to laugh.

What gives, cowboy? Are you trying to cause trouble?

Reid now understood the pens and paper Bree had delivered. "Do you mind taking a note back?"

Bree looped her arm through Madison's. "We were given strict instructions to wait until you had one for us."

Reid pulled the lid off the pen, twiddling it between his fingers while he thought of what to write. He had to be cryptic but sweet or Bree would get suspicious.

I just miss you. That's all. If our booths can't be side by side, at least I can keep an eye on you from way over here.

He drew a little heart and signed his name before folding into a square that he handed to Bree. The girls took off, giggling.

This time, Derek lagged behind for a second. "They are loving this."

"I'm glad. If you guys want to stop by in about ten minutes, I'll have another message ready."

Derek nodded. "See you soon."

* * *

AFTER SELLING a dozen donuts and passing a few more balloons and notes, Reid decided it was time to amp up his plan. He grabbed one of the balloons and carried it over to the table himself. By this time, they had an equal number of balloons on either side of the room.

"Excuse me," he said, ducking past a student while he slipped around the table to stand by Millie's side.

She beamed at him when he wrapped his arm around her waist.

"Thanks for the balloons." She looked like she was holding back a laugh. "Were you getting a little bored over there?"

"Nope. I just missed you." He looked up as the students in the front of the line gave a collective squeal.

Pink danced across Millie's face. It was time for Reid's final plan. He leaned in close, taking a moment to whisper in her ear. "I saw Mr. J circling your table. Is he a potential partner or can we make him jealous?"

Millie's breath tickled his ear when she answered. "He has asked me out almost every week since we started working together. It isn't always for a date, but the guy doesn't take a hint."

"Perfect. Then let's give him a sign he won't be able to ignore."

Reid stepped back and reached for Millie's hand. He spun her in a circle before pulling her close. Then he dipped her back, smiling when she popped her leg straight up in the air.

"Miss Millie Grant." Reid was using his ranch voice, speaking loudly enough to draw attention to them. "Will you do the honor of being my date to Grad Night?"

He set her upright, resting a hand loosely on her waist.

The expression on her face was difficult to read when she studied Reid's eyes. In the beat it took before Millie answered, he was afraid that he had pushed her too far. There were posters all over the cafeteria advertising the event, but Reid didn't know if teachers even went.

Reid's stomach dropped when Millie stepped away. He had crossed a line. He was getting ready to apologize when he saw Millie reaching for a marker. She shifted her body to block his eyes from what she was writing, but the kids near the front began to whisper back and forth.

Millie folded the paper into a small rectangle. Reid's hands were sweating when Millie came back to his side. She pressed the paper into his hands with a smile. He tried to steady his hands while he unfolded it.

The note held one word. *Yes.*

Reid paused for a moment. Then he held the paper high above his head, turning back and forth so everyone in the room could read it. "She said yes!" He turned his attention back to Millie. Her eyes shone bright with laughter.

They had certainly made their relationship public, but Reid wanted to really drive it home. He pulled her close enough that the top of her head tickled his chin. Then he leaned down and pressed a kiss to the top of her forehead.

"Thanks, teacher."

"Any time, cowboy."

The moment was over, but Reid headed back to his table, confident that he had done his part to ensure that the entire school knew about their relationship. Anyone that tried to set Millie up now would look like a cheater.

The event was drawing to a close when Bree brought another note to Reid. This one was folded like a button-down shirt. His heart kicked up a notch when he read Millie's words. *Before we go home, can I show you something?*

A secret rendezvous with the teacher at her own school? That sounded rebellious.

Bree was waiting for an answer. Reid grabbed a blue pen and wrote his reply.

You can show me anything you want. I can't wait to hang out.

He watched Millie's face when she read his response. This time, when she met his eyes, the playful laughter had been replaced with a more serious expression. She gave him a quick smile and mouthed the words thank you before turning back to her final customers of the day.

Reid's table was already out of donuts. He stacked the plastic trays in a pile and sent them to the kitchen with one of the students. The plastic tablecloth that covered the table was coated with sticky bits of glaze and sprinkles. He wadded it into a ball and tossed it in the trash on his way to Millie's table.

She was handing a metal cash box over to a man with

graying hair around the temples. The man looked up when Reid approached.

"You must be the man who was making a spectacle of our event."

Reid glanced at Millie. Her lips were pressed together in a thin line. "Reid Matthews, Sir. And you are?"

"Mr. Albertson. Principal of this school." He held his hand out.

"It's nice to meet you. And yes, I may have sent Millie a few balloons. Was that a problem?"

Mr. Albertson smiled. "I think it kept the teens happy, and happy teens tend to behave better." He patted the top of the cash box. "I'll take care of this. Thanks, Miss Grant."

Millie's expression didn't change until Mr. Albertson had moved to the next table. Then she reached for Reid's arm. "Let's go to my classroom."

If Reid and Millie were dating for real, her classroom would be a perfect place to sneak in a few kisses while no one was watching. Reid wasn't sure what to expect as she pulled him down the hall. They certainly weren't heading for a make out session.

It wasn't until Millie pulled the door behind them that Reid began to worry. Her face fell.

Reid stuffed his hands in his pockets. "Did I go too far today? That Mr. J guy seemed like he was trying to corner you, and I was stuck on the other side of the room."

Millie gave a gentle smile. "It isn't that. Can I tell you something that could potentially be construed as petty gossip?"

Reid leaned against the edge of a desk. "Of course."

The silence in the room grew thick while Millie fidgeted. She pulled her hair down, shaking it around her face before wrapping it back into a bun. Reid wasn't sure if she was ever going to speak.

"It's the principal."

"Mr. Albertson?" Reid was confused. Was Millie about to tell him that she had a crush on the principal? He didn't seem like her type at all.

"Yeah. I'm pretty sure he's stealing money from the school."

Reid let out a low whistle. "You weren't kidding about it being gossip. What makes you say that?"

Millie slid to the floor, her back resting against the wall. She pulled her legs in, wrapping her arms around them. Reid couldn't stay towering over her. He walked over and sat down, leaning forward slightly so he wouldn't bash the top of his head on the marker tray.

"It's all the little things. At first, I wasn't paying much attention. We were running out of supplies, and I figured it was a stocking issue. Then field trips started being canceled. The money the kids earned today was supposed to pay for a band for Grad Night in a few weeks, but I'm not sure they'll actually get the funds."

"What makes you say that?"

Millie leaned her head back against the wall and closed her eyes. Her hands were clasped together in a tight ball. "It's a gut thing. According to Mr. Albertson, the treasurer was sick, and he came to collect the cash boxes for her. I don't think I believe him though."

"Can't you just text her and ask if she is feeling okay?"

Millie shook her head. "It won't matter. He is going to walk off with the money any minute. If he's really stealing it, there will be no way to hold him accountable."

Reid's mind was spinning. He didn't know Millie all that well, but he thought he knew her well enough to be a fairly good judge of her character. She didn't seem like the type that would jump to conclusions without a just cause.

A real boyfriend would be willing to stand up to Mr. Albertson, confronting him directly to ask about the money. Reid couldn't take that chance. It wouldn't help his reputation to have people gossiping that he started fights at school. There had to be a different way.

"What about the kids?" He ran his hand through his hair.

"Are you asking if I told my students? I'd never do that."

Reid placed his hand on Millie's knee, pressing down for comfort. "I'm not accusing you of that. I was just thinking that they were kind of my secret weapon today. What if we send Bree and her friends to intervene? They could ask Mr. Albertson to teach them how he counts the money. If he does it in front of people, you'll know how much is supposed to be submitted to the bank."

It was a shaky idea. Reid knew he'd be able to get Bree to agree. The harder sell would be Mr. Albertson. He needed to be pinned down so he couldn't weasel his way out of it. Reid wasn't entirely sure why Millie was suspicious, but in the end it didn't matter. This was a simple way to make sure all the finances were okay.

Millie nodded. "We don't have a lot of time."

"Then we'd better get going." Reid helped Millie to her

feet, and they took off down the hallway. He pulled his phone out, shooting a quick text to Bree.

Can't explain, but gather your friends. Let's see how much money you made for the event.

He waited a beat for her text to come through.

Yay! See you in the gym.

The teenagers would be waiting. Now all Reid had to do was figure out how to trick Mr. Albertson into counting the money in a public place. The gym doors were straight ahead when Reid thought of a plan.

He reached for Millie's hand. "Do you trust me?"

Millie nodded. "I don't have much of a choice."

Reid was determined to make things right. "It's okay. I know what we have to do."

CHAPTER 10

Trusting in other people came pretty naturally to Millie, but she didn't know what Reid was thinking. All she knew was that he had an idea and going with a little bit of a plan seemed like a far better choice than going in blind.

"What do you need me to do?" Millie could feel their chance to stop Mr. Albertson slipping away.

"Just follow my lead."

Reid pushed open the doors and reached for her hand, pulling her towards Mr. Albertson. The principal was already surrounded by a dozen of Bree's friends, who were excitedly chatting. There was a strained look on his face, like all he wanted to do was go home and get a break from the kids.

"Please count the money right now so we know if we can hire the band. They said they'd save us a spot if we called them today." Madison was clasping her hands in front of her.

"Yeah. Can't you tell us the total before you take it to the bank? We want to know what we made." Derek was standing near the back, but his voice was louder than the rest.

Mr. Albertson rubbed his head. "It doesn't work that way. All this money isn't pure profit. You know that expenses will have to be taken out."

It was a fair point. The students looked at each other.

Millie gulped. This was her chance to make sure the money stayed where it belonged. "I heard what the kids were asking. I'd love to know how much we made too. We had a budget for the expenses, so I know what we have spent."

Purple splotches were filling Mr. Albertson's cheeks. "That just isn't the way we do things. You need three staff members to count the money, and as you can see, there's only Miss Grant and myself."

"I'm here, too," a voice called out. Mr. J straightened up with a cupcake wrapper in his hand. "I'm pretty curious, myself. It felt like we had more people here than last year."

Millie gave Mr. J a smile, even though she could feel Reid tensing up next to her. His hand slid across her shoulders as he pulled her close. It was cute that he was doing his job, but Millie was more focused on getting Mr. Albertson to be accountable for the money.

The principal was caught. He glanced at the stack of cash boxes in the wagon, and then back at the crowd. His eye twitched but then he straightened up. "I really wish we could, but there are too many people around. It just wouldn't be smart to count the money in this big of a crowd."

As much as Millie hated to admit it, he was right. It didn't make sense to count hundreds of dollars in a room that had strangers walking through.

"Don't you have an office?" Reid asked.

Bree chimed in. "There's the school library. You could lock the door behind you, or we could stand guard to make sure no one comes in."

They weren't wearing him down fast enough. "Sorry, guys. It's not how we do things."

Millie's heart was sinking. She didn't have any reason to doubt Mr. Albertson's words, but her gut told her that something was off. It was a shame to have worked so hard only to have a portion of the money stolen.

She glanced around the room at the faces of the teenagers who had gathered. In the grand scheme of things, Grad Night wasn't going to be a big deal. They'd go on to college, church missions, service trips, or even marriage, and Grad Night would become a distant memory. But right now? Grad night was closure to an incredible year. The kids deserved the best.

Mr. Albertson wasn't going to budge. All Millie could do was hope that he remembered his integrity when he walked off with the cash boxes.

The principal cleared his throat. "Well. If there's nothing else, I'd better get these somewhere safe."

He was turning to leave when Reid's voice rang out. "What if I double it?"

The room fell silent as all eyes turned to the cowboy.

Mr. Albertson's eyes narrowed. "I don't understand. You're volunteering to double the profits, even though you have no idea how much money is in these boxes?"

By now, parents had joined the crowd.

A woman with a blonde pixie cut pushed her way through to stand near Reid. "I can't match all the funds, but I'd like to help. I'll match the funds from one of the boxes."

She looked around the room. "Who else? Does anyone else want to help make this Grad Night the best one yet?"

Millie watched as Derek's parents stepped forward. They weren't affluent by any means, but they also didn't seem to be struggling for money like some of the other families in town. "We'll sponsor a box. If you count it right here, I'll write the check today."

The students were beginning to whisper to one another.

A tall muscular man pushed his way forward until he was standing by Madison's side. He jerked his head towards Reid. "I'm not going to let my buddy Reid have all the fun. I'll sponsor two of the boxes."

That was the final nudge the parents needed. Within minutes, every box had been claimed. Millie couldn't believe it. All eyes turned back to Mr. Albertson.

His cheeks lifted, but none of the smile reached his eyes. He looked like a cornered animal that was ready to explode.

"So, Mr. Albertson. What do you say?" Reid still had his arm around Millie's shoulders. She was going to be remembered for this event, good or bad.

The principal rubbed his head again before he let out a dramatic sigh. "Let's count some money."

The students let out a cheer, and everyone in the room divided into small groups. Millie was left standing alone with Reid and a very tense Mr. Albertson. Anger was rolling off him in waves, but he didn't say anything.

There was a brief moment where Millie worried that she was going to get fired on the spot. She leaned against Reid's side, grateful for his strength. It was time to get away from the ticking time bomb.

"Can I have everyone's attention?" Millie let out a sharp whistle and the people turned to face her. "I'll be here at the front of the room to keep track of the totals. Once you have your box counted, bring the cash to Mr. Albertson. He'll lock the boxes away for safekeeping."

Mr. Albertson gave a thumbs up. He was putting on a good face, but Millie knew they had pushed him pretty far.

"Once your box is turned in, bring the results to me. I'll add everything up and have a grand total for you once everyone is done counting."

Millie's body was shaking when she walked over to her booth to sit down. Thank goodness the janitors hadn't put all the chairs away yet. She sank to the chair, hyper aware of Reid standing beside her.

"What did I do?" she whispered.

"I'm pretty sure you just saved Grad Night." Reid slid a chair close and sank down next to Millie. He rested his hand on her knee, and Millie allowed herself to get lost in the butterflies. If this was how he acted around a fake girlfriend, how incredible would he be with a real one?

Millie's spirits lifted as the totals began to come in. The first box came from a booth that had sold cake pops.

Derek's dad stepped forward. "Our total came to $372."

Reid started laughing beside her. "That was from cake pops? No way."

Derek's dad winked. "There may have been a little extra money thrown in the pot. I figure my son will only be a senior once."

Gratitude flooded Millie's heart. Thanks to the generous donations they had already received from the community, the first cash box alone had covered their remaining expenses for the event. Everything else was going to be a profit.

"Thanks again for the support. You've got an incredible kid, there." Millie was beginning to understand why Derek had so many fans. His dad had the same charm as his son.

There was a small line queuing up behind Derek's dad. Reid reached for the next paper. His eyes were wide when he handed it to Millie.

"$473 from cotton candy." He shook his head. "There is no way that is accurate." The woman with the pixie cut grinned. "I couldn't believe it myself. I guess this table had a donation cup out and a lot of people tipped them."

"Thanks for saying you'd match it," Reid said. "I thought I was going to be the only one."

"I don't recognize you. Do you have a student that goes here?" The woman was sidling up to Reid while giving her hair a flirty toss. Millie turned to the side to hide a smile. Reid was only her fake boyfriend. She wasn't going to stand in the way if someone real came along.

Reid took Millie's hand and lifted it to his heart. "My sister goes here, but I'm not actually a parent volunteer. I just came to help this beautiful teacher."

The woman smiled and took a step back. "I'm hoping we get you for class in a couple of years, Miss Millie. I've heard great things about you."

Millie beamed, both from the compliment and the way Reid stuck to their rules. Rule two, hang out in public, was going great so far.

It was time to turn her attention back to the people in line. Donations were pouring in, and they hadn't even seen the bigger booth totals yet.

Millie bumped Reid's knee with her own. "How did you think about doubling the donations?"

Reid shrugged. "I've been around my fair share of alpha males. I knew if the stakes were high enough, he'd back down."

"But what if no one else had stepped up?"

Reid looked at Millie, holding her gaze until her pulse began to race. "I said I would double the donations that came in. I meant that."

She was the first to look away. Reid was handsome, but that was only the surface of the man. He cared about his family. He was a man of his word. And now, she was learning that he was incredibly generous.

"Well, you're off the hook now. The parents really stepped up."

Reid opened his mouth to speak but Madison's dad walked up. "Are you guys ready for this?"

"How did they do, Gary?" Reid held the pen, ready to write.

"The sugar cookie booth? They made $193 which I doubled to $386."

Millie rubbed her hands back and forth on her pants. "Huh. I thought they would bring in more."

Both the men were looking at Millie like she was crazy.

"Uh. Almost four hundred dollars on cookies is pretty good to me." Reid patted her arm. "Maybe the sugar fumes in the air are going to your head."

He was right. Millie laughed. "Don't get me wrong. That is a great amount. They were just our biggest earners last year." The sugar cookies by Sheila always went for a high price.

"Well, I'm not sure how the other booths compared, but the highest earnings came from the cupcake table."

"That's your table," Reid said. He gave Millie a high five before turning to Madison's dad. "I may have helped with those a bit. What did they earn?"

Madison's dad handed over a slip of paper. "After I doubled the amount, we ended up with $704."

Millie couldn't believe it. She had hoped the dozens of cupcakes she sold would be a hit, but she didn't have any idea they'd do so well. "Thanks for your incredible donation. I know the kids will appreciate it."

There was only one more box to be accounted for. The woman who handed her the receipt had manicured nails that were painted pink with white dots on them. "I didn't like the total we got so I added a bit."

Millie's eyes began to water when she looked at the amount. "A thousand dollars? Are you sure?"

The woman nodded. "I own the salon down on Main Street. I can count the donation as a tax write off."

"I don't know how to thank you." Millie's heart was overflowing. She looked up into the faces of the people surrounding her table and remembered she still had a job to do.

The salon owner smiled. "You can thank me by telling me what the students earned today."

Reid was tapping numbers into the calculator on his phone. He bit the end of the pen he was writing with, and then added the numbers again.

The anticipation in the room was palpable. Millie could feel the pressure of the students riding on her shoulders. Whether Mr. Albertson had been planning on stealing the money or not, this had turned out to be the best fundraiser ever. There would be plenty to cover the band for Grad Night, with the rest spilling over to the homecoming dance next year.

"I'll be back in a second." Reid stood up from the table, the paper with the totals clutched in his hands.

"Where are you going?" Millie asked. "What is the total?"

"Sorry, folks," Reid said, addressing the room. "If you'll be patient for just another minute, please."

Reid disappeared into the hallway.

There had been plenty of times for Reid to slip out if he was thirsty or if he needed a bathroom break. Millie couldn't think of a single reason why he'd have to leave right when they were about to give the students a total.

Two minutes later, Reid was back at the table. He held a paper at his side.

"Who is ready for the totals?" he asked.

The students began to cheer.

"I think Miss Millie should do the honors." Reid slid the folded paper to Millie.

Her hands were trembling when she opened it. "Thanks to the generous donations of all the community . . ." Her eyes read the total, but it was wrong. "Hold on a second."

The students groaned.

Millie stood on her tiptoes to whisper in Reid's ear. "I think you did your math wrong. We made a lot of money, but there's no way this is right."

He rested his hand on her shoulder before trailing it down her arm in a trail of heat. "I triple checked my work. It is right."

His breath was warm against Millie's cheek, making it difficult for her to think. Rule number one raced through her mind. She wasn't going to fall for the guy, no matter how many shivers raced through her body.

Millie wanted to believe him, but she had been paying attention to the amounts of money that had come in. It didn't add up.

"Are you going to tell us the totals?" Bree called.

Reid's words tickled her cheek when he whispered in her ear. "I said I was going to double the donations. Did you think I would lie about that?"

He slid the paper from Millie's frozen hand and held it up in the air, waiting until the crowd stilled.

"Thanks to the last-minute donations from all these amazing people here, you guys raised $9478 for grad night."

The silence in the cafeteria was so quiet, Millie could hear her heartbeat in her own ears. Then the students began to cheer so loudly, she was sure the neighbors could hear them.

A surge of students and parents alike swarmed the table, where Millie and Reid were separated in a sea of happy people. Millie lost track of Reid. When she found him again, he was passing a paper to Mr. Albertson.

Somehow, against all odds, they had managed to not only save the money the students had earned, but they had quadrupled it. The cowboy had come through for her in a spectacular way.

Millie reminded herself that Reid had a sister at the school. Maybe all his support had come because he loved her. In the end, it didn't matter. They had gotten Mr. Albertson to do what Millie had wanted him to do all along. He had to be accountable.

As people began to file out, the surge of adrenaline began to wear off. Millie was ready to go home and reward herself with a couple of hours of reading. She scanned the room, looking for Reid so she could drive him home. When she spotted him, he was on the opposite side of the gym.

Across the room, she watched as a tall woman with

dark brown hair approached him from behind. She tapped Reid on the shoulder, and he turned.

Millie was expecting to see Reid shake her hand or give her a high five like he had been doing with parents and students alike. Instead, he did the last thing she expected.

Reid's face lit up. He picked up the woman and spun her in a circle, her legs flying out. They were laughing when Reid pulled her into a bear hug. He rocked the woman back and forth before giving her a kiss on the cheek.

Millie had seen enough. Somehow, in their negotiations to establish a fake relationship, they had forgotten to put in any rules about dating other people on the side. She glanced back at Reid. Maybe it was just a very friendly parent.

That was when Reid draped his arm around the woman's shoulders, pulling her close to his side. The grin on his face made it clear that this was someone he had feelings for.

There was no reason for Millie to be upset, except that Reid was ruining the image they had carefully worked on all morning. No one was going to believe she was dating the guy if he was walking around with a gorgeous woman on his arm.

Sure enough, Mr. J was heading in her direction. Millie was a number of things, but she refused to be a woman scorned. Reid looked comfy enough with his mystery woman. He could get a ride home with her.

She ran to her car and pulled out of the parking lot as

fast as she could. The tears didn't begin to fall until she was speeding down the freeway.

It didn't make sense.

Millie knew she was in a fake relationship. She had promised that she wouldn't get attached or clingy if he showed her attention. So why was it, as she turned into her driveway, that her body could remember the feel of his breath against her cheek while he held her close? Why could she smell his cologne even though he wasn't there?

Having integrity was an important part of Millie's life. She unlocked the door with a heavy heart. It had taken a couple of days, but she had already broken her contract with Reid. She had most definitely gotten attached.

She was going to have to call the whole thing off.

All she had to do was convince her heart to let him go.

CHAPTER 11

The aftermath of the fundraiser left Reid on a high. He had started off the day as a service to Millie. They were supposed to be acting like a couple to get the matchmaking parents and teachers at the school off her back. There wasn't much Reid could do working across the room from her, but he thought they'd pulled off a pretty good bluff.

Helping to make the principal accountable was an extra bonus. For Reid, the best part had been watching how excited the teenagers were. Reid remembered his own Grad Night, and how awkward he had felt at the beginning of it. By the end of the night, the entire school was dancing together. He was glad Bree was going to get that experience.

The surprises kept going, because now Reid was hugging his sister, Hope.

"What are you doing here?" he asked. Hope wasn't due home for another week.

"I finished my finals early." Hope's gray eyes sparkled. "You didn't think you were going to have all the wedding fun without me, did you?"

Reid laughed. "You are more than welcome to the wedding planning. All I've done so far is get in the way."

Hope tried, unsuccessfully, to hide a smile. "I may have heard a little story about some chickens and a wedding veil?"

He ducked his head. "That was supposed to be a secret."

Hope squeezed her brother's waist. "I've heard a few things that are supposed to be secret, lately."

"Oh yeah? Like what?"

Reid waited while Hope scanned the crowd. He could already tell what was coming next. Sure enough, after a minute Hope turned back to face him.

"Where's the teacher?"

Reid feigned innocence. "There's a lot of teachers at this school. I think I saw Mr. J walk by a few minutes ago."

Hope elbowed him in the ribs. "You think you're hilarious."

"That's because I am." Reid knew exactly who Hope was talking about. He wasn't sure if he was ready to introduce her to Millie yet. Then he remembered rule two. If he and Millie were really dating, he'd have already found Millie and introduced her to Hope.

The sisterly interrogation wasn't going to stop. "I can't remember her name. Miss Lilly?"

Reid was saved from answering when Bree pushed him to the side so she could give Hope a hug.

"Hope! I can't believe you're finally here. Will you help me figure out how to wear my hair for the wedding?"

Even though the sisters were eight years apart, they were still close. "I can't wait."

Reid took advantage of the temporary distraction to scan the room. He had gotten separated from Millie after they announced the Grad Night totals. He had been so busy shaking hands, he had forgotten his duty to be a good boyfriend. He had no idea where Millie had gone.

Reid was pulling out his phone to text her when Bree grabbed his arm.

"Hope wants to meet Millie. Where did she go?"

"That's a good question. I haven't seen her in a while." Reid wasn't worried until he saw the look on Bree's face.

"You've lost your girlfriend? The gym isn't that big."

Reid shrugged. "True. Maybe she had to grab something from her classroom."

Hope looped her arms around her siblings. "Then let's go find her. I want to meet the woman who is making you smile so big."

Reid didn't have the heart to tell his sister that it would be a short-lived relationship. The point of the subterfuge was to paint a convincing enough picture that everyone would believe them, even if it was a lie.

They headed for the hallway. Walking out of the gym felt like someone had turned off the radio. The noise level immediately dropped to a faint roar.

"Have you been home yet?" Reid asked.

Hope shook her head. "I was heading there next. I

wanted to come here first to catch you with your new woman."

Reid stopped and planted his hands on his hips. "Alright. Which one of the siblings has been gossiping about me?"

Hope mimed zipping her lips shut.

Bree was trying to keep a straight face beside her.

"It's Porter, right? He's the biggest gossip."

Bree's hands flew to her mouth as she tried to hold back her laughter.

Reid stepped in front of his sister, crossing his arms. "It wouldn't be you, would it, Bree? Surely you haven't betrayed your older brother who just earned your school a lot of money, have you? You wouldn't do that."

Bree was laughing in earnest. "I may have snapped a few photos of you and Millie together."

"And then your phone accidentally leaked them to Hope?"

Hope pulled out her phone. "You guys look really cute together. I had to come check her out for myself."

Reid grabbed his sister's phone, swiping through the images. He had to admit that Hope was right. Bree had managed to capture moments where Reid thought no one was looking. There were pictures of him handing Millie the last balloon, and even a photo of him kissing her forehead.

His heart sped up. He knew it was just a fake relationship, but the couple in the photos looked like they were falling in love. He felt bad for lying to his sisters.

They were getting close to Millie's classroom. Reid's

hands began to sweat. He was going to have to sell the relationship in front of the girls. Hopefully Millie would play along.

His mouth was dry when they pushed open Millie's door.

The room was empty. Reid looked at the wall, where he had sat with Millie an hour before. She had been vulnerable with him in a way that tugged at his heart strings, which prompted him to take action. Now, he was missing her presence.

"Let's go check the gym again," Bree said. She took off down the hall, with a more subdued Reid following behind.

He was curious about where Millie had gone. It wasn't like her to disappear. As much as he was worried about passing her off as a legitimate girlfriend to Hope, Reid was also worried that maybe Mr. Albertson had done something. Was Millie in the principal's office getting fired?

They were almost to the gym when Mr. J passed by. Reid reached for his arm to stop him. "Have you seen Millie?"

The tennis coach had seemed interested in Millie's whereabouts all through the fundraiser. If anyone knew where she was, it would be him.

Mr. J puffed out his chest, straightening up so he was eye to eye with Reid. "She left about fifteen minutes ago. I'm not sure what happened, but she didn't look too happy."

Reid thanked the teacher and headed for the parking lot. If what Mr. J said was true, Millie's car would be gone.

He couldn't believe that she would ditch him like that. Not after he had helped her to make the event such a success. He must have missed something.

The parking lot had thinned out enough that Reid could tell Millie's car wasn't there. She had been his ride home. How could she leave him stranded?

He turned to Hope, pushing his irritation to the side. "Well, I guess you won't be meeting Millie today. Can I hitch a ride with you?"

Millie's disappearing act seemed completely out of character for her, but what did he know? He was just pretending to date the woman. If she was upset, would he even recognize the signs?

He sent Millie a text on the way home, asking if she was okay.

Her terse response left his stomach in knots. **I'm fine.**

The short answer gave him all the information he needed. He may not know her heart, but he knew women. In his experience, the words "I'm fine" meant that the woman was anything but fine. Somehow, he had messed up.

* * *

REID DIDN'T START to feel like himself until he was sitting in the tractor, the sound of the metal arm scraping against the dirt. This was his favorite backdrop. He could handle crowds, but now he was in his happy place. He needed the warmth of the sun beating against his back and the smell of dirt surrounding him.

As the metal teeth of the tractor dug into the earth, Reid waited for the feeling of being unsettled to go away. Millie's face kept popping up in his mind. She had been elated when she saw the amount of money they had earned for the school. Somehow, that elation had turned into her ditching him at the school. Now she was ignoring all his text messages and phone calls.

Reid wasn't sure what he was supposed to do with that. In making their rules, they had planned for fake scenarios. They didn't talk about what to do if someone was genuinely upset. Then again, he wasn't sure if she was even mad at him. Maybe she needed to get home to take care of Rex. Or there could have been a family emergency. She even could have spilled punch down the front of her dress.

None of those situations would explain why Reid was getting the cold shoulder. He shifted gears, turning his attention to the job at hand. The nice thing about fake dating someone was that it really didn't matter why Millie was upset. She wasn't his problem to deal with.

He tried to push Millie completely out of his mind, but no matter what he did, she kept popping up in his thoughts. She wasn't his girlfriend, but he liked to think they were at least friends. And he wasn't the kind of guy who ditched his friends, no matter how much they pushed him away.

If Millie wasn't going to talk to him, he was going to figure out why. He just had to finish plowing the field so he could put on something a little more presentable.

The sun was dipping close to the mountains before Reid was finally ready. He showered and changed into a new pair of jeans before he pulled a clean shirt over his head. The guy facing him in the mirror looked confident. That was a man who could mend fences with the woman he was still getting to know.

The nerves didn't start to kick in until Reid pulled up to the front of Millie's house. He reached for his water bottle, taking a long sip to wet his suddenly parched mouth. The car was shaking from his knee bouncing up and down.

Reid would run into a herd of stampeding cattle if he saw someone in danger. This was different. He was about to knock on a door with no warning about what he was going to face. How did you prepare for danger when you had no clue where the danger was coming from?

He pressed his hand down on his leg to stop the bouncing. The time for stressing was over. Was he going to sit in the car like a coward or face the music?

Reid was many things, but he refused to be afraid. He took a final swig of water and slammed the lid shut on his water bottle. It was time to knock on the door.

Millie's front porch was decorated with a flower wreath. Tucked between the branches were small birds. He hadn't paid any attention to how the porch looked when he visited the night before. Now he had ample time to study every detail because Millie wasn't answering her door.

In his determination to make things right with Millie, Reid had genuinely forgotten that the woman might not be home. He slid down so he was sitting on the concrete steps, debating about what to do. The last thing he wanted was for her to think he was stalking her.

That was his answer. Reid was going to have to try again another day. He stood and dusted off his jeans.

"Are you going somewhere, cowboy?" Millie's voice appeared out of nowhere, startling Reid.

"I thought you were gone." Reid gave his jeans a final pat and straightened up, looking towards the road to see where she had come from.

Millie's cheeks were deeply flushed. Her hair was twisted back off her neck in a simple bun. Instead of a button up blouse, she was wearing a pair of leggings and a lightweight mesh jacket that accentuated her curves.

"Were you jogging?" Reid's eyes flicked up and down her body, landing on her running shoes.

"It was just a quick run to clear my mind. Why are you here?"

Reid cleared his throat. "You said you're fine, but I don't think I believe you."

Millie stepped towards the porch and propped one foot up on the step, leaning forward in a stretch. "Are you calling me a liar?"

That was a direct hit. Reid smirked. "Maybe. Really, though, I'm calling myself insecure. I thought we had a great day together, but somehow, I found myself stranded in a parking lot with no ride home. It makes it hard for me to believe that we are okay."

Millie nodded. "Sorry about that. I figured you'd hitch a ride home with your girlfriend."

Reid snorted. "Aren't *you* supposed to be my girlfriend? I thought that was the whole point of this."

Millie paused, mid-stretch, and pinned Reid down

under the weight of her glare. "Me too. It's a little difficult pretending like I'm your girlfriend when you are snuggled up with another woman." She took a deep breath. "Look. I realize we never talked about what would happen if either of us met another person. I'm certainly not going to stand in your way. I'm also not going to stick around and watch you cheat on me. I have better standards than that."

There were words coming out of Millie's mouth, but none of them were making any sense.

Reid hooked his thumbs through his belt loops. "I'm not following."

"I saw you with a woman. You guys looked pretty chummy together. And let's be honest. She was gorgeous. I can see why you'd choose her."

There had been several women at the fundraiser, and Reid had talked to quite a few of them. He wasn't flirting with any of them though. And Millie had no right to be upset. She had talked to plenty of men through the day, including the very persistent Mr. J.

"I'm confused." That seemed to be the safest sentence to lead with because Millie was clearly on edge. Reid ran a hand through his hair. "You wanted me to show up today, right?"

"Yeah."

"And we ended up raising a lot more money than you'd thought we would, right?"

Millie was bending down to touch her toes. "Yeah. We raised enough to cover the live band. The rest will go to the student budget for next year."

"So, tell me why you'd be mad that we were getting

congratulated by people. You shook just as many hands as I did, and I'm not calling you out for cheating."

Millie straightened up, her arms flying across her chest as she crossed them. "Shaking hands? You think I'd be mad at you for shaking hands?"

Reid shrugged. "I mean, aren't you?"

"No."

The clipped answer reminded Reid of why he had come in the first place. They had promised to have fun with the fake dating but standing on Millie's porch felt anything but fun. He was missing something.

Reid had a choice. He could stand on Millie's porch, never learning why she was upset, or he could head home. He knew better than to fight a losing battle.

"You know what? I'm going to head out. I promised my sisters I'd meet them for ice cream, and I'm not going to keep them waiting."

"Your sisters? Bree's the only one here."

Reid started walking towards his car. "Hope got home this morning. She's going to be here until the wedding."

He was reaching for the door handle when Millie's hand flew to her mouth.

"Hey Reid," she called. "Does your sister happen to be tall with long brown hair?"

Reid paused. "Yeah. She looks like all of us."

"So basically, a prettier version of you?"

Click, click. The pieces were starting to come together. "She's definitely the pretty one. I can't tell you the number of guys she's had pining after her."

Millie was walking towards him. "Did she show up at the fundraiser today?"

Reid couldn't hold back his mirth as he put together the final piece. His fake girlfriend had been jealous of his sister? Her anger made a little more sense. "Yep. She came there to surprise me."

There was contrition in Millie's voice when she leaned against the side of his car. "So, she's the woman I saw. Rule four. No getting attached. Rule five. Have fun. I kind of blew through both of those rules today, didn't I?"

Reid nodded. "I mean, kind of. I couldn't figure out what I had done wrong."

Millie rested her hand on Reid's arm, her fingers warm against his skin. The gesture felt more intimate without dozens of eyes watching them.

"I'm sorry." Millie rubbed Reid's arm. "I let my pride get in the way of our contract. Can we try again?"

Millie had broken two rules, but Reid was ready to forgive her. A cool breeze was dancing through the trees when he decided to break a rule of his own. With no one around, he should be keeping his distance. Rule three said to only show affection when they had to. He didn't care. He wrapped Millie in a hug. A friend could do that, right?

"We've still got a wedding to get through. I'm game if you are."

Millie's answering grin when he stepped back was all he needed.

"I know it's late, and you probably have a million teacher things to do, but do you want to come to ice cream with me and my sisters? Hope really does want to meet you."

He held his breath, suddenly caring more than he anticipated about what her response would be.

"I'd love to, but I'm a mess. I don't want the first time I meet your sister to be when I'm sweaty and gross from jogging. Raincheck?"

"You've got it."

Reid climbed into his Mustang, his heart much lighter than it had been when he left. They just had to make it five more weeks until the wedding, and then the ruse would be over. They could fake it for that long.

CHAPTER 12

When Millie was younger, she had blushing contests with her friends. The goal had been to see who could make the other person blush first. All it had taken was Hazel mentioning the name of Millie's crush, and Millie was out.

Now her cheeks were filling with heat over a guy that she didn't have feelings for. Sure, he was easy on the eyes, but that was it. Millie watched him drive away, schooling herself for letting his impish smile get to her. Her red cheeks had more to do with how she had treated the guy than how she felt about him. He had hugged his sister, and she had turned into a jealous monster.

Millie needed to clear her head. She glanced at her calendar when she walked in the house. Five more weeks until Hazel's wedding. There would be a couple more dress fittings and a rehearsal dinner, but those would be in a large group. If Millie played it right, she'd be able to keep her heart in check until she and Reid could fake break up.

Millie stood in the shower, grateful for the water that cascaded down her body in streams. She took slow breaths in and out, letting her worries wash down the drain. By the time she got out of the shower, she was centered again. The weekend counted as a win. Millie could let it stay that way without worrying about complicated feelings.

She was clearing off the table when she saw a folded piece of paper that made her pause. It was one of the notes Reid had passed her. The edges were crumpled from being in her pocket, but it didn't matter. His cute words were part of a game that made their relationship very public.

The notes weren't something she needed to save, but she paused to read each paper again before she got rid of them. As the papers fell to the trash can, Millie's stomach filled with butterflies. They weren't the most important notes of the fundraiser. The most important note was the one where she had scrawled three large letters across the paper in response to Reid's question.

Had she really said yes to a Grad Night date with the cowboy? She was going to have to add shopping for a new outfit to her list, along with a better shield for her heart. Reid had been charming enough at the fundraiser, but the fact that he had taken the time to make sure she was okay? That was absolutely endearing.

It had taken less than a week, but Millie had already jeopardized their fake relationship by breaking the rules. She wasn't going to do that again. Especially not with the wedding so close.

Millie got out a pen and started making a list of her own. Ways to avoid getting a crush on the cowboy. She had known the guy for a week and already her mind was drifting to him. That wasn't going to do.

Rule one: No daydreaming about how it feels to have him wrap his strong arms around you, or how good he smells when you rest your head against his chest.

Rule two: No texting back and forth unless it has something to do with your next public appearance. And no hoping for more appearances just so you can sneak hand holding in.

Rule three. No thinking about the mischievous glint in his eyes or the way they crinkle when he's happy. No fantasizing about how it feels to be the one who makes those eyes shine.

Millie tapped her pen against the table. She was a teacher who taught creative writing. She could tell her students how to craft an epic love story, but she couldn't tell her heart how to behave. In the end, it didn't matter how her heart felt. She had agreed to a carefully constructed set of fake dating rules, and she was going to make sure she honored them.

Huffing, Millie crinkled her paper into a ball and tossed it in the trash. She was going to have to do better than writing down a few rules if she wanted to stay true to the promises she made to Reid.

* * *

BY THE TIME the sun was rising the following morning, Millie's emotions were back to normal. She had slept through the night without any cowboys riding through her dreams. In fact, the first person she thought of when she opened her eyes was her sister. She hadn't talked to May for over a month. It was time to check in.

It was past nine o'clock in the East, but May's phone went straight to voicemail. Millie debated about what message to leave, but she hung up before the beep. There was no way she could wrap up the events of the weekend in a short message.

Millie took the time to fry up hash browns and eggs. She carefully placed her plate in the center of the table, just out of reach of Rex's curious nose. Once she poured a glass of orange juice, she was ready to dig in. Pulling the plate close, Millie opened her phone to scroll through messages while she ate.

Usually there were a couple of messages from students or parents, asking for clarification about a project or an assignment. This time, Millie found dozens of messages in her inbox. She groaned in anticipation of what could have made so many people reach out. Had she forgotten the link for the homework assignments again?

Taking a deep breath, Millie opened the first message. It was from a person she didn't recognize, thanking her for the fundraiser. Millie clicked to the next message, her heartbeat slowing. The message was similar to the first. Another grateful parent had reached out.

By the fifth email, Millie was bouncing in her chair. Somehow, in less than twenty-four hours, word had spread about the money they had raised. Mr. Albertson wasn't going to be able to steal any of it. Not without someone noticing.

It took Millie another fifteen minutes to reply to all the emails, her breakfast pushed to the side. She leaned back in her chair when the final reply was sent, turning her phone over in her hands. It would be easy to go about her day, ignoring the fact that there was another person responsible for the outstanding success of the fundraiser. Reid already got his congratulations the day before.

That wasn't the type of person Millie was. She sent a quick text, her fingers flying over the keyboard. **I've gotten lots of emails this morning from happy parents. Thanks again for your help.**

Reid's answer came through seconds later. **It was all you.**

Millie lunged across the table to pull her plate away from a drooling Rex. She was dropping it in the sink when another text came through. **But I loved watching it unfold.**

Reid was being modest. If he hadn't volunteered to double the money, the entire event would be under a cloud of suspicion. Millie really needed to get to the bottom of what was happening with Mr. Albertson. She should be able to trust the guy.

Giving her plate a final shake, Millie dropped it into the dishwasher. She texted Reid a quick response. **Let's give both of us credit. In the end, the real winners are the kids.**

She set her phone to the side and pulled out her laptop. Thanks to the fundraising event, she was behind with her grading. There were still fifteen papers waiting to be read.

Millie was skimming the first paragraph when her phone began to ring.

Reid's name flashed across her screen. With a smile dancing on her lips, Millie answered.

"Congrats!" Reid's happy voice sent the butterflies swirling through Millie's stomach.

"Thanks. I'm glad we pulled it all off."

"Me too. Anyway, I was checking to see if you wanted to come to family dinner tonight."

Reid's words sent a wave of panic through Millie, effectively dousing her butterflies. She swallowed, trying to ignore the lump in her throat.

"I was planning on getting caught up on my grading today." It was an honest answer. She did have to get caught up.

Reid gave a low chuckle. "What's more important? Your real job or our . . ." He lowered his voice. "Fake relationship?"

Millie relaxed the vice grip on her phone. "Well, one of them certainly pays better."

"You're talking about the fundraiser, right? I'm sure at least half of those sales were because of the cute balloons I sent you."

"I'm sure you're right." Millie was laughing now. "What time is dinner?"

"Five o'clock, on the dot."

The computer screen was filled with essays that needed to be graded, but Millie knew if she put her mind to it, she'd be ready in plenty of time. "Can I get back to you?"

Reid's chuckle flowed through the phone. "No pressure.

Just let me know later if you're going to make it. Otherwise, Bree will probably keep gossiping about you."

That was a threat worth thinking about. Millie grinned. "I'll text you later, cowboy."

"Good luck with the grading, teacher."

The phone screen went blank, and Millie turned back to her reading, trying to ignore the butterflies which were beginning to dance in her stomach again.

* * *

BY THE TIME the afternoon rolled around, Millie was running out of excuses for avoiding dinner. She had graded the papers, finalized lesson plans for the week, and even found time to clean the bathroom. With each tick of the clock, she could feel the walls pressing in around her.

At 4:15 Reid sent a text. **Thoughts on dinner? Yes or no?**

Millie's finger hovered over the button before she began to type. **I'll be there.**

She pushed her phone to the side like it was a hot poker. Now there were no excuses left. By the end of the evening, Millie would know if Hazel believed that she was dating Reid.

The hour before Millie needed to leave flew by in a blink. She found herself standing on Reid's doorstep, hands shaking as she reached out to knock on the cheery yellow door.

Reid threw the door open with a grin while he reached

for Millie. "Play along," he whispered as he pulled her close. "They are all watching."

Millie schooled her features into a grin. "I've been waiting all day to see you," she said. She gave his back a quick rub before turning to face his family.

Now that the siblings were standing side by side, Millie felt foolish for ever thinking Hope was anyone other than family. She bore a striking resemblance to her brothers and sister, with the same dark hair and beautiful eyes. There were definite differences, like Hope's eyes being gray instead of brown, but the similarities were there.

Millie's mouth went dry when Reid cleared his throat. "Introduction time. Let's get this out of the way." He lifted his hand towards his mom. "Mom keeps this ranch in line. As much as she'd hate to admit it, she loves having some of us around to harass her."

Mom Matthews grinned and held out her arms. Millie was enveloped with the smell of fresh herbs when she hugged her. "I'm glad you're here."

Reid wasn't leaving time for any side conversations. He plowed through the remaining introductions, barely giving Millie time to say hi. "You know Porter, Emily, Thomas, Hazel, and Bree."

Millie nodded. These were all people she had met, albeit briefly, at the dress shop.

"And finally. This is my sister, Hope. She's back from school for a break."

"I've heard a lot about you," Hope said.

Millie forced her voice to be relaxed. "I've heard a lot about you, too. You're studying the performing arts?"

Hope bumped Reid with her hip. "This guy got it right for once. Performing arts is my major, but I'm minoring in education. I figure I'll give my music a go first. I'll teach high school music as a back up if my career doesn't take off."

"That's right. I forgot you were a singer." Millie admired anyone who could sing in front of an audience. She froze in front of crowds. "Once your fame wears off, I have connections at the local high school. I'm sure you'd make a great teacher."

Hazel looped her hand through Millie's arm. "Let's get to the table before the rest of the inquisition begins." She rubbed Millie's arm, leaning close so she could whisper in her ear. "Relax. They seem like a lot, but this is actually a really good group once you get to know them."

Millie let Hazel lead her to the dining room, aware of Reid following right behind. He pulled out her chair for her before taking his own seat. The family bowed their heads in unison as Thomas began to pray. After a resounding amen, the family passed around dishes filled with delicious food until every plate was piled high.

Reid sliced through a piece of sliced roast on his plate. Millie's heart began to race when he winked at her. "Ready?"

Without waiting for an answer, Reid turned to the family. "Alright guys. Let's get this over with. What do you want to know?"

Millie froze by his side.

"Relax," he whispered. "If we get through this, we're in the clear."

Millie forced herself to take a measured breath. "You're right."

Hope smiled at Millie from across the table. "Where did you meet?"

Her question was immediately followed by Porter's. "How long have you been dating?"

Millie pressed down on Reid's leg. "I've got this."

It was time to get fully initiated into the family. "Reid and I met at an underground dog fighting ring. I was trying to break the dogs out when I heard a movement. I turned to see a tall man standing behind me. He asked what I was doing, but I was too scared to answer. In the end, it didn't matter. Reid put two and two together and grabbed the metal cutters from my hands. We were freeing the last dog when the alarms began."

Reid was laughing. "It was awful. Alarms blaring, dogs barking, and in the distance, we could hear the roar of the crowd. Millie and I barely escaped."

Bree's eyes were wide when she looked across the table. "Did you get caught?"

Porter shook his head at his brother before he flicked his sister's hair. "Of course not, silly, because there is no way that story is true."

Hazel had tears of laughter running down her cheeks. "I can't believe you just told that story."

All the eyes at the table turned to Hazel.

"Have you heard it before?" Thomas asked. "Is it the plot of a movie or something?"

Millie shook her head. "It's the beginning of a short story one of my students wrote a few years back. Hazel and

I had a bet going for how many times we could tell that story." She grinned at Hazel. "Looks like I win another point."

"So, he didn't save you." Bree sounded disappointed.

Millie looked up at Reid, with true gratitude in her eyes. "He didn't save me from getting caught, but he did help save our school."

She leaned back in her chair and let Bree take over the story. As she watched the faces turned towards Bree, Millie's heart opened. This was a family that cared for each other. They were going to hate her when they realized everything was a ruse.

Reid held a hand up. "To be fair, I was only there for the final parts of the day. Without Millie's help, the fundraiser wouldn't have even happened."

Bree's eyes lit up. "I still can't believe how much we made." She paused to take a sip of water. "The best part is that you guys are going to Grad Night together. You'll get to hear the band."

Hazel choked on her water. "You're what?"

Millie was caught now. She smiled, giving Reid's hand a squeeze. "He asked me to Grad Night, and I said yes. I was planning to be there as a chaperone anyway. Now I'll be there, chaperoning with this handsome guy by my side."

"And I'll get the final dance with her." Reid held Millie's gaze, his eyes making a slow loop from her eyes to her lips.

Hazel nudged Thomas. "Want to double with my best friend and your brother? I'm sure they could use more chaperones."

Warning bells were ringing in Millie's head. If Hazel

and Thomas were there, it was going to be so much harder to pretend like she and Reid were falling in love.

"I'm not sure," Millie said, but Reid's voice was louder.

"That would be awesome."

Reid's warm hand gave Millie's shoulder a reassuring squeeze.

She hid her sigh. "I'll check tomorrow to see if there are any spots left." All she could do was hope that miraculously, all the spots had filled.

It was time to move the focus off her and Reid. Millie turned to Bree. "Are you going to Grad Night? Even though you're not a senior?"

The smile that filled Bree's face warmed Millie's heart. The young girl was definitely smitten with someone.

"Derek is taking me. Just as friends."

Porter's laughter filled the room. "Keep telling yourself that, Bree."

Millie could tell there was a story there, but she was going to have to get Reid alone to hear it. She knew Derek from her class. If he was Bree's date, a lot of girls were going to be jealous.

Millie was stabbing asparagus with her fork when Bree cleared her throat. "Back to you, Millie and Reid." She turned to face Millie. "Have you guys kissed yet?"

CHAPTER 13

*R*eid hid his smile when Millie's cheeks blazed bright red. Clearly, she wasn't ready for Bree's direct hit. "Come on, sis. That isn't a fair question. I didn't ask you if you've kissed Derek yet."

It was Bree's turn to blush. "You're the worst."

Reid needed to steer the conversation to clearer waters. "We're taking things slow. I'm not in a rush to get married like these buffoons over here."

Porter laughed. "You just wait. Your time will come."

The conversation moved to the topic of wedding cake flavors and Reid felt Millie's leg relax beside him. She leaned towards him, and he bent down so his ear was close to her mouth.

"Tough crowd," she whispered.

Reid put his arm around her chair, grateful that she was willing to sit by him at all. "You'll get used to them."

His words were meant to reassure Millie, but he felt a pang of remorse. He was asking her to get to know his family, but when they broke up, she'd look like the bad guy. Reid had to ensure that he took the fall, and not Millie. Especially since his sister went to her school. Millie didn't deserve to have rumors flying about her.

The rest of dinner went off without an incident. There was a lot of good-natured teasing, like most large families had, but the conversations stayed light. Reid was glad his family was behaving.

After dinner, Millie cleared her throat. "Thank you for a lovely evening. I should be heading off."

Bree pushed her chair in. "You're not staying for game night?"

Reid's stomach clenched. He had forgotten to warn Millie about family game night. That was something a real girlfriend would know. Sure enough, the faces were turning towards Millie.

Hazel was the first to speak. "You love games. Why don't you want to stay?"

Millie was trapped. Reid stepped to her side, eager to jump in, but the answer was already rolling off her tongue. "You know how competitive I get. I don't want to ruin everyone's first impression of me." She winked at Reid. "I wanted to stay, but I have to finish a few things before school starts tomorrow. The fundraiser took up a lot of my weekend."

Mom Matthews stepped forward and placed her hands on Millie's shoulders. "I'm so glad you took time out of your busy schedule for us. It was great to meet you."

Hope pushed her way forward. "I hope you can stay for games next time."

Reid slid his arm around Millie's waist, steering her away from the family. "I'll be back in a minute," he said, looking over his shoulder at his siblings. He kept his arm around Millie until they turned the corner, where he quickly dropped it.

"You were amazing back there." Reid's entire body was relaxing. They had actually tricked his family.

"I feel bad lying to them." Millie's eyes were somber. "They're a great group."

As much as Reid hated to admit it, he had to agree. "I keep reminding myself that they are going to get over their disappointment when we break up. They can't expect me to marry the first woman I bring around."

They were standing in front of the door. Millie turned to face him, her eyes going soft. "Am I really the first woman you've brought home?"

It was Reid's turn to feel embarrassed. "I haven't found anyone worth it, yet."

"Interesting."

Millie's one word answer had Reid's mind churning. He wished he could read her thoughts to know if she was feeling judgment of pity.

He turned the doorknob, swinging open the door so Millie could walk through. She remained silent as she made her way to the car. Their relationship had been filled with lighthearted banter, but now Reid felt like he was doing something wrong. Was it possible that Millie had already had enough of him? Maybe the white lies were getting to her.

Reid wasn't ready for their time together to end. Not

when their conversation felt so stilted. "Can I show you something?"

Millie lifted her eyes to his and he saw a tender smile that passed so quickly, he was afraid he had imagined it.

"Sure."

His heart was thumping when he led the way down a short hill. Branches from a weeping willow tree were hanging over the path. Reid held them to the side so Millie could pass through.

"Just a little farther." Reid said. He held his hand out to help Millie climb down a steep incline, releasing it quickly so he wasn't breaking the physical touch rule.

"Remember the chickens who played with Hazel's veil?"

Millie nodded. "I didn't meet the offending party, but I'll never be able to get that picture out of my mind."

Reid headed towards a pile of boards leaning against the side of an old barn. "I guess they weren't done causing mischief. Look what we found yesterday."

Nestled between the boards and the tall weeds was a momma hen surrounded by chicks. The little fluff balls were hopping around in the grass, their high-pitched chirps filling the air. Millie squealed when she saw them. "They are so tiny. Why are they here and not in the main barn?"

"We collect eggs every day, but sometimes one of the hens finds a great hiding spot. Miss Whithers totally tricked us. We're letting the chicks get a little bigger before we introduce them to the rest of the family." Reid reached into a tin can and pulled out a scoop of grain. "Do you want to feed them?"

"Yes!" Millie's wide smile caught Reid off guard. She reached for the scoop. "Is there anything I need to know?"

"Nope. You can scatter it however you'd like. The chicks love to hunt for the grains."

Millie took a pinch of food off the top of the scoop and threw it near the chicks. Her laughter was contagious as the chicks darted to the food, scratching the ground as they pecked at it. Millie tossed a few more pinches of food, scattering it around the weeds before she tossed the remainder of the grain to the ground. "What about their mom? Can she live off this stuff?"

Reid pointed to a small dish tucked off to the side. "We put out oyster shells for mom so she can get enough calcium. Otherwise, she's fine."

A warm breeze kicked up, blowing through Reid's hair. He watched Millie, taking in the happy smile on her face. Millie reached down to gently stroke one of the chick's small heads.

"Thanks for showing me these guys." She straightened up and looked at Reid. "Why did you want to?"

Worry clawed at Reid's insides. "I wanted to make sure we were okay before you headed home."

"Dinner wasn't as bad as I expected. Your family is great."

Reid nodded. "I think that's my problem. I got so caught up in the fake dating thing, I didn't think about the impact it would have on the rest of the people we know. Are we bad for leading them on?"

In response, a chick hopped up and began pecking at Reid's shoelace.

Millie rested her hand on his arm, pulling his focus back to her. "Do you want to break up?"

The relationship was fake, but Reid's heart felt heavy at the thought of ending things. "I don't know. What about Grad Night? My invite wasn't exactly subtle."

"Definitely not." Millie leaned against the barn wall just as a beam of sunlight broke through the clouds, highlighting hints of deep brown in her black hair. Reid knew, whatever they decided, he wasn't going to be able to get the image of her out of his mind.

She was beautiful. In any other universe, Reid would ask Millie out for real. He had his honor though. He was going to fake date her, pushing all his feelings aside, no matter how pretty she looked standing against the barn, because that is what he promised to do.

Millie's brow furrowed and Reid's stomach sank. Her eyes were unsure. Then they softened. "How do you feel about keeping up the ruse for a little bit longer? At least through Grad Night? It would be really nice to get Mr. J off my back permanently."

She was saying the words he hoped to hear. If the last date he ever had with Millie was a high school event, he was going to make the best of it.

"Let's do it."

* * *

THE NEXT TWO weeks flew by. Whenever Reid entered the house, he knew he had a fifty-percent chance of getting approached by one of his sisters. Hope had jumped right into the wedding planning. She was often found sitting at the kitchen table with ribbons spread around her.

"Can't you hire people to decorate for weddings?" Reid asked while he cleared a small space on the table for his lunch plate, pushing loose pieces of ribbon to the side.

"You can, but where would the fun be in that?" Hope picked up another small piece of ribbon. "Besides, these are decorations for Hazel's bachelorette party. We're not going to hire that out."

Reid rolled his eyes at his sister, but once he was finished with his lunch, he moved everything back to its original spot. "They will look great when you're done," Reid said.

He was grateful that Thomas's bachelor party was going to be much simpler. The guys were doing a campfire out at their cousin's ranch. They would come home smelling like smoke, but at least they wouldn't look like a glitter bomb had exploded all over them.

Reid headed out to the barn. He was putting a bag of fertilizer away when Bree found him.

"Are you ready for Grad Night?" She was bouncing on her toes, which meant that she was excited.

As silly as it sounded, Reid had to acknowledge the bubbles in his stomach. "I've got my dancing boots ready. I'm also kind of nervous."

"About what? Miss Millie seems great."

"She is. But we're going to be the old folks there. What

if we start rocking out to the band and you guys laugh us off the floor?" Reid didn't care what a bunch of high school students thought about him, but he did worry about Millie's reputation.

Bree began to laugh. "You'll fit right in. Last year my friend Lyndsey's mom and dad were chaperones. They were dancing the whole night. By the end of the night, we were dancing right along with them. I think my classmates are used to a little strange."

"So, you're saying we should be the center of attention . . ." Reid trailed off and looked at Bree, trying to keep his face straight.

"Don't you dare." Bree bumped his hip. "All I'm saying is that you don't need to be afraid of what we'll think. Everyone loves Miss Millie. I think she could serenade us off-key from the microphone and the students would still love her."

That was interesting to hear. He had guessed Millie was popular with the students, but it sounded like she was a favorite teacher. Hopefully he didn't mess things up for her.

The day of grad night Reid woke up with a queasy stomach. He ate a few bites of breakfast before heading to the fields. By the time lunch came around, Reid was worried he was coming down with a stomach bug. He headed back to the house in time to see Bree and her friends heading out. They were going horseback riding before Grad Night, which was a novelty for some of the kids. Bree could ride circles around Derek, but he didn't live on a ranch like she did.

Reid leaned against the front door while he watched his sister bantering with her friends. Derek held open the door for Bree, which earned him a couple of good points in Reid's book. Derek wasn't from one of the big ranching families, but at least he was a gentleman. Reid pulled out his phone and sent a text to Millie.

Did I mess up by not inviting you on a day date? I thought that was something people only did for school dances.

Millie's answer took a few minutes to come through. She put a row of laughing emojis. **You're good, cowboy. I know you have real work to do today. Some of the kids make a whole day out of the event, but we're not exactly kids anymore.**

She had a point. The knot in Reid's stomach loosened. **Just making sure. I don't want you feeling left out.**

Are you still picking me up at 6:00?

Reid took his hat off and hung it by the door. **Yep. My mom was giving me a hard time about not getting our picture together. Think Rex can take one?**

Another laugh emoji came through. **I'll ask him. He doesn't have the best track record though.**

By the time Reid was tucking his phone in his pocket, he was beginning to feel a little better. He was looking forward to seeing Millie that night, even if it was for show. He dug into his lunch, the churning in his stomach ebbing away. Their date was going to be fun, even if he did make a fool of himself.

* * *

FIVE HOURS LATER, Reid was standing in front of the bathroom mirror, styling his hair while Bree banged on the door.

"Are you almost done?" Bree's strained voice belayed her urgency.

Reid gave his hair a final pat before swinging the door open. Bree stood in the hall, rocking from side to side while her hand steadied a delicately twisted bun at the back of her head. "We ran out of bobby pins. Hope's checking the other bathrooms while I check this one."

Even with her hair a mess, Reid felt a swell of pride. "You look beautiful, Bree." Reid held open the door for her while he walked out. Derek better treat her right.

Bree's grateful smile reminded Reid why she was the favorite. "Thanks. You don't look so bad yourself."

He pulled at the end of his tie. "You don't think the tie is too much, right?"

"Honestly? We're all going to be pretty casual. You could ditch the tie."

"Got it."

Reid left the bathroom to his sister and headed back to his bedroom where he pulled off the tie. He slipped out of the dress shirt and into a short-sleeved, plaid button-down, grateful for his sister's advice. Dressing casually was going to make the event much more comfortable.

Reid's palms were sweating when he arrived on Millie's doorstep. He rapped on the door and stepped back while the sound of Rex's loud barks filled the air. Millie's muffled shush instantly quieted the feisty dog.

When she opened the door, Reid let out a low whistle. "Looking good there, Teach."

Millie's dark hair was pulled up in a simple ponytail, highlighting her slender neck. Instead of her usual business casual, she was wearing a pair of jeans that hugged her hips. Scrawled across the front of her light green t-shirt was the sentence, *I'm silently correcting your grammar.*

Reid busted up laughing. "You're really driving this teacher thing home."

Millie pulled a key out of her purse and locked the door. "I figure this is one of the last times I'll be seeing some of these kids. I want them to smile."

"I'm sure they will." Reid tucked his hands in his pockets before he could reach for her hand. It was getting harder and harder to deny his growing feelings for Millie. Holding her hand felt like a natural step, but it was against their rules.

The drive to the school was much too short. Millie was telling Reid about one of her favorite students when they pulled into the empty parking lot.

"Thanks for volunteering to help with setup. We've got about an hour before the kids start to arrive."

"You said there would be parents here tonight as well?"

Millie nodded. "They've done most of the work already. Our job is to wait for the band and help them with whatever they need."

Reid shut the engine off and turned to face Millie. "How did you get involved with this? I don't see a lot of other teachers jumping in."

Millie's voice grew soft. "This event matters to all of us.

My first year of teaching, there was a group of seniors who started celebrating their graduation early. They snuck a couple of bottles of whiskey from one of their dad's offices. During the middle of the night, one of the more inebriated students decided to drive home."

"I can see where this is going." Reid's stomach clenched. He had heard these stories before. They never ended well.

"There were a lot of miracles that evening. The boy swerved into oncoming traffic but overcorrected his path at the last second. Instead of crashing into a minivan filled with a family of seven, he crashed into a telephone pole."

Reid could picture the accident, the car crumpled like an accordion. "What about the kid?"

Millie's pain filled the car. "The car was totaled but he made it out alive. After a couple of weeks in intensive care, the boy was able to head home. That accident changed him, physically and emotionally. He has a permanent limp to remind him of that day."

She paused, her voice getting stronger. "We came together that year and decided that we never wanted any kids to get in that position again. This Grad Night event was started the following year. We give the graduating seniors a safe placc to celebrate their accomplishments, but unlike a lot of schools, we let students from all the grades attend. No alcohol or drugs are allowed. The idea is to make this event the best place to hang out tonight, so they don't want to be anywhere else."

"So that's why the fundraiser mattered so much to you." Reid looked at Millie, seeing a new side of her. He was starting to understand that there were a lot more layers to the teacher than he had expected. If he didn't reign his heart in, he was going to ruin everything with her.

A truck pulling a trailer drove into the parking lot, interrupting their conversation. The trailer was painted red, with large white lightning bolts streaking down the side.

"That's got to be our band," Millie said. "Are you ready?"

"I hope so. Let's go."

Reid followed her across the parking lot, sternly lecturing his heart to slow down. The only thing that mattered in the moment was getting the band set up so the teens in the town could be safe. That was a job Reid was more than happy to get behind.

CHAPTER 14

Setting up the band went far quicker than Millie imagined. She had pictured lugging around guitar amps and untangling microphone cords. Instead, the lead singer handed her a couple of cords to tape down and the band took care of the rest.

The good news was that they were set up much earlier than they needed to be. The bad news was that Millie was left standing next to Reid when the band launched into their warmup, a loud, upbeat song giving way to a swoony slow tune that pulled at her heart.

Her mouth was dry when she realized that Reid was standing close enough to her that she could feel his breath against her cheek. All it would take was her turning to the side and she'd be in his arms, swaying back and forth in time to the music. She knew how those arms would feel when they wrapped around her waist. Reid would hold her firmly, forming a protective cage that would keep her safe.

That wasn't going to do.

"Let's, uh, check on the snack station." Millie tried to keep her voice steady, but she made the mistake of glancing at Reid. He looked away, hiding his smile before he turned back.

"Again? I'm pretty sure the table is full, with hundreds of extra treats stacked in the kitchen." He pressed a hand to Millie's arm and heat ricocheted through her body. Trailing his hand down her skin, Reid reached for Millie's hand.

He gave it a gentle squeeze. "Millie, I haven't ever been on the planning side of an event like this, but from where I'm standing, it seems like you're ready. The kids are going to have an incredible night."

Millie's eyes darted around the room. Reid was right. Everything was in place, from the playful red and black decorations hanging from the ceiling to the table piled high with food. There were plenty of volunteers milling around, waiting for the event to begin.

She wanted to relax, but Reid's thumb was marking a lazy circle on her hand. Every nerve ending of her body was hyper aware of the man standing beside her, trying to comfort her, his calloused hands gentle against her skin. Millie decided to let her guard down. She leaned into Reid's chest, smiling when his other arm wrapped around her shoulders, pulling her close.

"What if it's not enough?" Millie lifted her eyes to meet Reid's.

There was fire in his eyes, which he quickly blinked away. "It's enough. The kids are going to have a great time, and they are going to be safe."

Reid slid his hand to Millie's back, tracing a large circle between her shoulder blades. The heat of his hand left trails of warmth behind. "Why are you worried?"

It was getting difficult to form coherent sentences. "Because we messed it up one year and another kid got hurt."

Reid pulled back, taking his warmth with him. Millie stepped out of the bubble, cold water dousing her skin. She was letting herself get caught up in the fantasy of the moment, but the real work of the night was about to begin. There were over one hundred students attending, and Millie's job was to keep every one of them safe.

"That wasn't your fault." Reid held her at arm's length. His eyes blazed with conviction. "Unless you handed the kids alcohol while they were leaving, they were responsible for their own actions. You can't save everyone."

Millie wanted to believe his words. She wanted to go back to the lighthearted banter that formed their fake relationship. Her heart swirled with emotions as she remembered the day they made their rules.

A chill trickled down her spine. Rule four. Don't get attached. She was acting like a clingy girlfriend who needed comfort. Not like a mature woman who was seeking the advice of a colleague.

Millie shook her shoulders and Reid dropped his hold. "You're right. I'm overreacting. Thanks for talking me through it."

Reid opened his mouth to speak but Millie cut him off. "It looks like Mrs. Monterey is waving us over. Let's go."

She led Reid over to the front table where all the volunteers were gathering, shaking off the feeling that she had just had a close call. The dating rules were in place for a reason. If only she could ignore the fluttering in her stomach long enough to remember what that reason was before she fell completely in love with an impossible match.

Mrs. Monterey took so long assigning everyone to their stations that Millie's heartbeat was able to return to normal. She was breathing steadily when she headed towards the drink station with Reid following behind.

"Thanks for agreeing to help at the school again," Millie said. "I'm not sure this is what you were expecting when we made our agreement."

Reid's eyes were laser beams that held her in place. "There are a lot of things I wasn't expecting when we made that contract." The unsaid words frightened Millie. She knew what she hadn't expected. She hadn't expected to develop real feelings for the cowboy. She had only known him for a few weeks, but he had invaded her thoughts. Her life was better with him in it.

What if he felt the same? There were several ways to find out what Reid was implying, but Millie was hesitant to ask. She didn't want to look like all the other women who were smitten with the guy just because he was handsome, charming, and the sweetest gentleman ever.

"Like what?" Her words came out as a whisper. "What weren't you expecting?" Millie wasn't sure that she wanted to hear the answer, but she wasn't going to let fear ruin her night.

The hesitation must have been written across her face

because Reid reached for a stack of cups, pulling them an inch forward. "It's not important. Do you think this will be enough cups?"

Changing the subject was a safe action to take. Millie made a show of examining the tall stacks, pretending like she cared more about the objects in front of her than the complicated feelings swirling through her body. As far as the cups went, there were more than enough. If things went according to plan, they wouldn't have to restock anything for a couple of hours. As for her mind? That was going to take a little more work.

Millie gave Reid's hand a gentle squeeze. "I think everything is going to be fine." She hoped he could hear the double meaning behind her words. The drink station was going to be fine, but so were she and Reid.

Her calm lasted for less than a minute. Millie bent down to pick up a napkin that had fallen to the ground and jolted up as Reid's hand dropped around her waist.

"Mr. J sighting on your left," Reid whispered.

Millie's hand instinctively flew to cover Reid's. "Let the games begin."

Reid's reassuring squeeze was all the answer she needed. She began laughing, doubling over before she straightened up and wiped a tear from her eye. "That was hilarious."

Mr. J stood in front of their table. "Did I miss something?"

Millie leaned into Reid's embrace. "Reid was just telling me a story about his brother."

"Huh." The words were clipped. Mr. J pushed the cups

back into place. "I was checking to see if you guys needed any help. Looks like you two lovebirds are set over here."

Reid held his hand out. "Thanks, man. We've got it covered." He shook Mr. J's hand before wrapping his arm back around Millie's waist.

Millie didn't let her breath out until Mr. J was gone around the corner. "I swear, that guy just can't take a hint."

Reid turned her so she was facing him. "How much do you want to sell our relationship?" He ran a hand through his hair. "I mean, I haven't really turned on the charm yet today."

Was the air suddenly thicker? Millie tugged at the neck of her t-shirt. If Reid had been holding back so far, Millie wasn't sure she was ready to see what the full-blown charm would look like.

"Bring it on." Millie drained a cup of juice in one gulp, crushing the cup to hide the shaking in her hand.

She watched Reid's face as he scanned the room. The last time they had been in the high school gym, he had delivered her a bunch of balloons. There was nothing like that in the room now. Just a crowd of students that was steadily growing.

"Got it. I'll be back in a sec." Reid left Millie's side, making his way over to where the band was waiting, their instruments in hand. Reid whispered to the lead singer before making his way back to Millie.

"Do you want to tell me what that was about?" Millie's palms tingled with anticipation.

"Nah. You'll find out soon enough." Reid's eyes lit up before something on the other side of the room caught his attention. He furrowed his brow. "There's Bree and Derek. What do you know about the guy?"

"I know that Derek is one of the most popular seniors at the school. He's going to break a lot of hearts when he heads to college in the fall."

"Are you telling me my baby sister is out with a player?" Reid's fists were curling.

Millie reached for his hand, feeling bold with her touch. She ran her fingers across his palm, gently caressing his hand until his fists relaxed. "From what I've heard, he's really a great guy. If it makes you feel better, I'd let my sister date him."

Reid looked down as if noticing Millie's hand wrapped around his for the first time. He lifted her hand to his lips, pressing a soft kiss to it. "I trust you. And I guess I'll reserve judgment for later."

"That's my man."

A loud screech filled the room.

"Sorry about that, guys." There was a man adjusting the microphone. He tapped it once and then set it in a stand. "Welcome to grad night! I'm Rocko and this is the band. Let's give it up for The Lightning Bolts!"

His words were met with cheers.

"How many seniors do we have here tonight?"

Several hands flew up. Millie was proud to see a large number of her students. The end of every school year was always bittersweet. The best part of being a teacher was getting to see the students as they grew but she was going to miss them.

Now the students were heading off to bigger and better

things. Some of them would stay in town, working small jobs at the diner or the gas station. Others would head out of state to college, where they would choose careers that would carry them through their lives.

No matter where they ended up, she could take comfort in the fact that for this night, at least, those students were going to have a great time in a safe environment.

"What do you say? Should we send these seniors off in style?" The crowd was cheering when the band began to play their first song.

Reid held out his hand. "Do you want to dance?"

The energy in the room was electric. Millie hesitated for the smallest of moments before she decided to throw out all caution. For Grad Night, she was going to act like everything was fine.

Reid led her onto the dance floor, pushing his way through the crowd until he found a spot near Bree. "This way I can keep an eye on Derek," he said, leaning close to whisper in her ear. Millie guessed he was only half teasing.

"They're going to be fine." Millie swayed her hips from side to side, keeping up with the tempo. She was ready to leave all the frustrations from the school year on the dance floor.

After a few upbeat songs, Rocko took the mic again. "Is everyone having a good time?"

Millie wiped her forehead while the crowd roared their approval. Her feet were going to ache by the end of the night, but it would be worth it.

"Let's take a beat to say thanks to the people who made this night possible. Everyone, clear the floor."

Students and chaperones alike pressed to the edges of the room, leaving the dance floor open. Millie held back a laugh. This was probably the first time all the students had listened to an adult without at least a couple of kids choosing to ignore the instructions.

Rocko nodded in approval. "Right. I'm going to need everyone adult who made this event happen to come to the center of the floor."

Millie's heart began to race. She preferred to stay on the sidelines, letting the students get the attention.

She followed Reid while he made his way through the crowd. Standing in the center of the gym with the other helpers, surrounded by students, Millie's heart was ready to burst. She had poured her heart and soul into teaching. Looking around at the individual faces, Millie knew it was worth every sleepless night she spent worrying if she had been doing enough.

Rocky nodded towards the volunteers. "This song's for you." He picked up his guitar and strummed the first few bars until the band joined in, a familiar slow song filling the air.

"Ready for that charm?" Reid winked at Millie before he gave a dramatic bow. He held his hand out, giving Millie a final choice if she wanted to take it. Even now, surrounded by students, Millie had the option to back out of their agreement. Looking into Reid's eyes, she knew what her answer would be.

"I'm in." Millie held her hand out, gasping when Reid quickly pulled her to his side.

"How's your waltz?" His voice sent a quiver of delight

through her that intensified when he slid his hand to the center of her shoulder blade.

"I know the basics," Millie said. She rested her hand just below his bicep, trying not to fixate on the muscles beneath the thin layer of his shirt.

"Perfect. Follow my lead." Reid clasped Millie's right hand and he stepped forward, leading her in a box step.

Millie began to laugh as they wove in and out between the parents. She should have guessed that somewhere in Reid's arsenal of wooing women, he would have learned to dance. If someone had told her that she would be waltzing at Grad Night with a fake cowboy boyfriend, she'd have laughed in their face. This was something she couldn't have predicted.

Spinning around the dance floor, bodies inches from each other, Millie let herself sink into the moment. Rule number one was out the door. No falling in love for real? That was impossible. Her heart was already heading down that road, and she didn't think she could pull it back. Not with the flutters racing through her entire body while Reid pressed her close.

After a couple of circles around the room, Reid spun Millie away from him. He was laughing when he spun her back. This time, instead of resuming their waltz, Reid began to sway from side to side. He pulled their hands in until Millie's palm was resting on his chest. Longing flooded her body when he lowered his hands to her waist.

The song ended but Reid kept dancing for another couple of beats. Millie closed her eyes, trying to capture every detail, from the song that had been played and the sound of the teenagers cheering to the heat that trailed from her hands to her cheeks. She leaned in, breathing in Reid's aftershave before she allowed her eyes to open.

Reid was staring at her with an intensity that was difficult to miss as his eyes flickered from her eyes to her lips. Was it possible that he was feeling the same emotions as she was? The gym faded to the distance as Millie studied his face.

His brown eyes held longing. Longing for their relationship to be something more than a farce. Millie held back a sigh when he let go of her hand. He clasped his hands behind her back, pressing against her waist. This was much better. She slid her hand up his shoulder to his neck, teasing her fingers through the back of his hair while she rested her other hand on his chest.

"Woot!" The cheering voice broke through Millie's haze.

"You going to kiss her or what?" another voice called.

Millie dropped her hands as if they were on fire, and stepped back, clearing her throat. "I, um." She took a deep breath and met Reid's gaze. "I need to check the drink station."

The crowd parted the way for Millie while she made her exit. She opened one of the drink dispenser's lids, peering inside before she closed it.

"I should probably, uh, mix more lemonade just in case." Millie gestures with her hands, not entirely sure who she was giving her excuse to.

A warm hand brushed against Millie's cheek. Reid was standing close. Too close.

"What can I do?" he asked. The quiver in his voice betrayed him. He was clearly fighting the same emotions she was.

For the first time, in as long as Millie could remember, her heart and her mind were in sync. She knew exactly what, and who she wanted. It was time to take control of the situation.

"You can follow me."

Millie headed towards the kitchen, not needing to glance back to see if Reid was following. She knew that he would be. One way or another, their contract was ending tonight.

The door clicked shut, shutting out the noise from the gym. Millie headed past the kitchen counter to a small alcove that wasn't visible from the door. She had a lot on her mind, and she didn't want any interruptions.

Her heart was racing when she turned to face Reid, but her voice was calm. "Reid. We need to talk."

CHAPTER 15

Usually, a clandestine meeting in the kitchen would be right up Reid's alley. Instead, the walls were closing in on him. He had almost slipped up and kissed Millie right there on the dance floor. Now he was being pulled into the corner so she could yell at him away from the watchful eyes of the students.

"I'm sorry," he began.

Millie held a finger to his lips. "It's my turn."

"But I can explain." Reid needed Millie to understand that he could respect her, even if it didn't feel like he was.

She held her finger up again, shaking it in front of his face. "I said it was my turn."

Reid's stomach sank. He wasn't going to get a chance to defend himself.

Millie's arms were crossed when she began to speak. "We need to break up."

Shards of ice doused his body. "But, you're not letting me explain. I'm sorry I got carried away with the dancing."

That earned a smirk. "Where did you learn to dance like that anyway?"

Reid straightened his back. "I needed an extra credit my freshman year in college, so I took a class. I'd heard the class would be filled with girls."

"I see. Were you right?"

He looked at the ground, willing it to swallow him whole. "That's not the takeaway from this. The takeaway is that I kind of fell in love with dancing. I haven't been able to do a lot of it since college. For what it's worth, you are a great partner."

Millie smacked his shoulder. "You're distracting me. This is why we need to break up."

"Because I like dancing?" That was an unfair reason to end things.

"Yes. Because you like to dance. And because I really like dancing with you. It's not just that."

Millie's hair was hanging in her face. Reid lifted his hand to brush it behind her ears. Then he froze. If they were really breaking up, he couldn't make up excuses to be close to her.

She carried on as if she didn't notice his hesitation. "It's everything. Dating you is living a lie, and I can't keep living this way."

Each word was a punch to Reid's ego. If he couldn't keep a fake girlfriend, how would he ever keep a real one?

"Can I say something?" Reid ignored his better instincts and reached for her hair, tucking it back into place.

Millie nodded.

"For starters, as much as I hate to let you go, I won't

hold you back." His heart was heavy as it struggled to push the blood through his body. "We agreed we could end this whenever we needed to."

"Thank you."

"But if I had a choice, I'd ask you to stay. Don't give up on me yet. I can reign it in."

Millie's face fell. "That's not the point."

"Then what is? You don't want me to do better?" Reid stepped back so he was leaning against the cool door of the refrigerator. His heart jumped when it began to hum loudly.

"The problem isn't you, Reid. It's me."

She was pulling out the most cliché break up excuse ever.

"I've heard that before. Why can't we keep up the ruse until the wedding?"

Millie looked away; her shoulders slumped. "Because I can't keep my promise to you."

She turned to face him, her voice growing stronger. "I can't keep lying to everyone around me, but I especially can't keep lying to you."

"What are you lying about?"

Reid studied Millie's face, waiting for her answer. He wasn't going to let her leave without a fight.

In response, she clasped her hands together. "It's the contract. Our stupid, five-rule contract. I'm struggling with some of those rules."

"Like hanging out together in public? I told you I'd work on it."

Millie looked up to the sky, taking a slow breath. "Rule

two. Hang out together in public so people can see us. The problem is that I want more."

Reid cupped his hand to the back of his neck. "We can do more. Are there any other school events you want me to go to? Or we could go on a couple of dates."

Millie shook her head. "That wouldn't work, because then we get to rule three. Only show as much affection as we have to."

All the moments Reid had reached out to Millie slammed into his mind. He had thought he was acting cool, but had he gone too far? He liked wrapping his arm around her, but he hadn't thought to check if she was comfortable with it. Maybe he had overstepped his boundaries.

Reid pressed back against the fridge, trying to widen the gap between them. "Did I cross a line? I'm sorry. I should have checked to make sure you were okay before I held you."

Millie's finger was up again, telling him to shush. "It's my turn to talk. The problem isn't that you've been showing me affection. The problem is that I like it. Kind of a lot. And I shouldn't."

She was talking faster and faster. "Rule four. No getting attached. I'm afraid I'm getting too attached to you, and I promised I wouldn't."

The conversation had taken a sharp turn. Reid's heart was beginning to race. "I don't know what to say."

Those clearly weren't the right words. Millie's face fell. "Exactly. You don't know what to say because we started this adventure together with a carefully crafted set of rules. You have been following the rules, and I haven't. It isn't fair to keep you in a contract that I can no longer follow."

She reached for his hand. "Thank you for giving me an adventurous few weeks. I didn't know how much I needed you, but I'm glad we met." There were tears in her eyes when she stood on her tiptoes and kissed Reid's cheek.

He closed his eyes, praying for the right words to say. When he opened them, Millie was heading towards the door.

"Wait," he called. Everything was moving too quickly. For the first time in years, he had finally found someone he wanted to spend his time with. And now he was watching her walk away.

Millie turned, her head upright. "I feel stupid enough. Can you just let me go?"

Reid watched the woman he was crazy about fighting her emotions and something in him broke. "No. I can't."

Tears streaked Millie's cheeks. She swiped furiously at them. Reid crossed the distance to her, taking large steps so he was at her side. He held his arms open, and Millie stepped into his hug.

"I can't let you go," Reid whispered into her hair. "Because I've broken some rules too."

Millie shook her head against his chest. "Not like I have."

"You don't know that." Reid pressed a kiss to the top of her head. "Rule four. No getting attached? I haven't been able to stop thinking about you since the day we counted the cash boxes. You were strong that day, fighting for what the kids needed."

Millie sniffed. "That's what teachers do."

"Some of them, yes. But not the majority. Everyone else at the fundraiser was willing to let things be, but you spoke up and ensured that the kids would be taken care of."

The refrigerator began to hum again, the dull rumble filling the air. "Look at today. How many kids are off the streets and partying in a safe environment because of your help?"

Millie didn't speak, but she nodded her head.

Reid pressed his hand against her back, steadying himself for what he had to say next.

"And while we're talking about the rules, what about rule one?"

With a click the fridge turned off, leaving the room completely silent. Millie pushed back from Reid's chest to look at his face.

"It's too soon for rule one." She shook her head.

"I agree." Reid smoothed down her hair. "Rule one says no falling in love for real. I'm not saying I'm in love with you, but I'm definitely falling into serious like. I personally want to see where this goes."

He held his breath, waiting for Millie to respond. Reid had never told anyone he loved them before. He wasn't entirely sure what that would look like, but he imagined that what he had with Millie was a good start.

Millie wiped away a tear. "I guess I kind of like you a little bit, too." She lifted her eyes to meet Reid's and his heart melted.

"What do you think about throwing out the old

contract and forging a new one?" Reid ran his thumb across Millie's cheek, wiping away one of her tears.

"Can we do that?"

He began to laugh. "I think it will be okay. We're the ones who made the contract, so if we both agree to break it, we should be good."

Millie nodded and stepped out of Reid's arms.

"Hey. I liked you where you were."

Millie pulled out her phone. "If we're going to make new rules, someone has to take notes."

"Alright. I'll allow it." Reid leaned against the steel counter, the cool metal anchoring him to the room. "Rule one."

Millie's cheeks flushed pink. Reid tried to hide his smile. "How about this? No pressure to put a label on our relationship."

"Even if we accidentally fall in love?" Millie's eyes held a teasing sparkle, but Reid's heart sped up.

"Even if we accidentally, or on purpose, fall in love." He waited while Millie typed into her phone.

"What else?" She glanced up from her notes.

"I think we were doing well with our hanging out in public. Would you agree?"

Millie nodded. "I'm not sure it needs to be a rule, but I'll make a note of it. The wedding is in three weeks, and I guess I could handle a couple more dates with you before then. But only if you're up for it."

Reid rubbed his hands together. "I have a few ideas."

"Should I be worried?" Millie looked up from the screen.

Reid rubbed his hands together. "What if for rule two we agree to take turns planning dates?"

"Got it. Rule two. We alternate who plans the date, and no fussing if you don't like what the other person chooses."

"Hey. I didn't say that." Reid pushed his sleeves up. "Does this mean you're going to take me to fairy tea parties and make me watch girly movies?"

Millie's fingers were flying across her screen. "Great ideas. I've got them down."

The fridge kicked on again, this time with a soft rattle that joined the humming. "Something's not right with that thing," Reid said. He peered behind the fridge, but he couldn't see much without pulling it away from the wall. He looked over his shoulder. "While you're putting ideas down, don't forget to add the Monster truck rally and going to the shooting range. Oh, and watching baseball games."

"I added them." She looked up with a smirk. "What makes you think I'm all fairy princess parties? I'll out cheer you at any baseball game we attend. And just wait until you've seen me handle a gun."

Reid raised his eyebrow. "Noted." He was enjoying his conversation with Millie, but in the back of his mind he knew they were shirking on their chaperone duties. There was still one subject he wanted to get some clarification on.

He slid his hands into his pockets. "I think we did awesome following rule five. I know I've had fun hanging out with you."

"Me too." Millie set her phone down.

"And I think we can agree that we both kind of destroyed rule four. I know I got kind of attached to you." Reid stepped towards Millie.

"Agreed." She dropped her eyes and reached for her phone, picking it up so she could fidget with the case.

"So, according to my calculations, that leaves us with rule three."

"Mmm hmm." Millie began to shift from side to side. "There's that rule. What do you want to do about it?" She lifted her gaze to Reid's.

Reid held her gaze, walking around the counter until he was standing in front of her. "I definitely have some thoughts." He reached for her hand, pulling her into dance position.

There was no music, but Reid led Millie in a slow waltz around the kitchen, bringing her back to the alcove that was away from prying eyes. He slowed their dance until they were swaying in place.

"I know I like the way you fit in my arms." He held her arm up and guided her in a spin, dropping both his arms to her waist when she was facing him again. "And I really like the feel of your waist against my hands."

Millie brought her hands up, so they were resting against his chest. He clasped one of her hands, pulling it to his heart.

"This is a good place to be. I know when I reach for you, you're going to sink into my touch. And when I brush your hair off your face, you're going to give me a little smile." He brought his hand to her cheek, running his finger along her jawline before he reached for her hair.

Millie's expression didn't change, but she leaned her cheek into his hand, parting her lips with a sigh. "I can't help it. You make me nervous, in the best sorts of ways. When you are near me, I know I want more."

Reid nodded, sliding his hand to the back of her neck where he lazily trailed his fingers back and forth. "How do you feel about a modification for rule three? Instead of only showing affection when we are out in public, what if I have permission to hold your hand any time you reach for mine? And what if I can wrap my arms around you every time you lean in?"

Millie's eyes were blazing when she slid her hand up his chest. "I think I can work with that. I hope you're ready for your arms to be constantly full, because I never intend to stop reaching for you."

A quiver of delight shot through Reid's body. He had hoped that Millie was feeling the same. "What happens when we get back to the gym?"

"Your hand is going to be in mine." Millie squeezed his hand for emphasis.

"And when they play a slow song?"

"You are going to slide your hands to my waist and I'm going to wrap my fingers in your hair."

The air was getting thick. Reid tugged at his collar, feeling flushed. "And when the dance is over, and I take you home?" He arched an eyebrow, waiting for Millie's permission to do the one thing he had been dreaming about.

Millie wrapped her arms around his neck, pulling his head towards hers. She stopped, inches from his face, and tangled her fingers in his hair.

"You'd better leave me with a kiss that makes me forget why we were fake dating in the first place."

Reid didn't hesitate. He lowered his chin the final inch and pressed his lips to hers. She responded with an intensity that made him wonder how he had made it as long as he had without kissing her. Their lips belonged together.

With a small grunt, Reid picked Millie up, not breaking their kiss when she wrapped her legs around his waist. He walked forward until she was pressed against the wall. The alcove was hiding them, but Reid wasn't taking any chances of getting caught.

He slid his hands to her hair, gently teasing loose her ponytail. The tie came loose, and her silky hair fell around his hands. Reid deepened the kiss, taking his time to taste the cherry lip gloss she wore. Every fiber in his body ached to pull her closer, so there was no space between them.

Instead, he broke the kiss and let her slide to the ground.

Millie's bright eyes stared up at him, her desire clearly written on her face. She bit the side of her lip. "Did I say you could stop?"

"I could stand here kissing you until the sun comes up tomorrow, but that's not why we're here. We do have some responsibilities, right?"

Millie growled. "You saw the same drink station I did. The kids are going to be fine for a few more minutes."

The implied command was one that Reid was happy to follow. He pressed his lips to hers, memorizing every detail of the way she fit against him. Millie wasn't the first girl he had ever kissed, but she was filling his heart with hopes and dreams that made him wonder why he had taken so long to kiss her in the first place.

Reid trailed a row of kisses along Millie's jawline, the smell of coconut and jasmine filling his nose. He was making his way back to her lips when the kitchen door banged open, and the sound of voices filled the kitchen.

"Hey, why are the lights on in here?" The voice came from one of the teenagers.

Millie pulled Reid close, burying her head in his chest like he could shield her from prying eyes. Reid pressed them into the corner of the alcove, praying that no one needed anything from the fridge.

"Don't know, don't care," another voice answered. "But I found the boxes of cookies."

There was a shuffling movement before someone hit the light switch and the room fell dark.

Reid remained frozen in place, hyper aware of the teacher he was protecting. She began to shake against him, a loud laugh escaping her lips.

"Oh my gosh. Did we really just make out in the school kitchen?"

Reid's lips were tingling with desire. "Yep."

"And we almost got caught." The dim emergency light that kicked on showed Millie's silhouette bent over. She gasped for air. "Now I get how those kids must feel every time we catch them."

The fridge chose that moment to start humming again, but now there was a loud rattle that was followed by a thump. Then the motor died.

"I'm guessing that's our cue that it's time to get back."

Reid opened the door to check that there was nothing inside the fridge. Then he slid his hand behind it and coaxed the plug away from the outlet. "Someone's going to want to take a look at that."

Millie reached for his collar, running her hand along the edge of it. "I'm not sure how I'm going to explain this one to the custodial crew."

"You could tell them that you were making out with a really hot cowboy in the kitchen when the fridge died."

She laughed and smacked his shoulder. "Not a chance."

Reid brushed her hair off her shoulders. "It's not as fun, but you could tell them we were looking for any extra refreshments." He opened the fridge and made a show of peering in. "I don't see anything."

Millie reached for the front of his shirt and turned him to face her. "One more kiss for the road before we get responsible again?"

Reid answered by pulling her close, sinking into the softness of her lips. They could throw the rest of the rules away because he was sure this was all he wanted to be doing for the rest of the evening.

When they parted again, Reid's heart was beating fast. He slid his hand to Millie's and gave it a gentle squeeze. That was where he planned to keep it for the rest of the night.

CHAPTER 16

When they walked back into the gym, it took a moment for Millie's heartbeat to slow. She was waiting for someone to point out the dreamy smile on her face, or comment on how her eyes reflected the giddiness she felt inside. Instead, all eyes were turned to the stage where the band was continuing their set.

Millie slid closer to Reid's side so she could discretely straighten the hair on the back of his head. That was a bad idea, because her fingers remembered how it felt to be playing with his hair. Her cheeks warmed at the thought. There would be time for kissing later.

As the song shifted to a slower beat, Reid pulled her to the dance floor. This time, with the floor full of students, he settled for a gentle, old-school swaying. They rotated in a slow circle, getting closer to the band with every turn.

The song was ending when they reached the front of the stage. Reid rested his chin on her head for a beat before kissing her forehead. Millie closed her eyes, wishing the song was longer. The final notes faded, and the crowd began to cheer.

Millie was happy the kids were enjoying themselves. She didn't realize she and Reid had drawn so much attention until the crowd began to chant.

"Kiss her, kiss her."

She held her hands to her cheeks to hide her blush, but it didn't matter.

The kids were chanting louder now. "Kiss, kiss, kiss."

Reid arched his eyebrow. "Should we give the crowd what they want?"

Millie knew this was the last time she'd see a number of these kids. If they wanted to see her happy, who was she to say no? She nodded and lifted her chin.

In response, Reid dipped her low to the ground, her hair brushing the floor before he pulled her halfway up. He leaned his body forward to make up the distance and kissed her gently on the lips before pulling her all the way up.

Students were cheering all around them, but Millie only had eyes for Reid. He had kissed her much harder in the kitchen. This softer side to him was somehow even more endearing. The man clearly knew his audience. As much as the high school kids wanted their teacher to be happy, they certainly didn't need to see her making out with anyone.

Happiness wrapped Millie in a cocoon. She had started the month being paired up for a wedding with a guy who wasn't able to commit to a relationship. She was ending the month officially dating Reid and feeling more secure than ever in their relationship.

Millie's euphoric bubble carried her through the late hours of Grad Night. Long after the party was cleaned up and the kids were heading home, she was still floating.

* * *

HER FRIENDS NOTICED her mood the following week. They had gone to breakfast to celebrate school officially being over.

"Alright, Millie. What gives? Why are you glowing?" Steph was staring across the top of her stuffed cream cheese French toast.

Millie shrugged. "I'm always happy at the end of the school year. You know how it is. The last couple of weeks are hard, but then in the fall I get a new batch of kids to look forward to."

"Yeah," Dawn said. "But this is different. You're happier than normal."

Hazel lifted a hand to her mouth to cover a smile.

"You know something, don't you?" Steph stabbed a strawberry, swirling it through syrup before she popped it in her mouth.

"I'm not saying a word." Hazel's eyes were sparkling. "But if I had a guess about why our friend here is so happy, I'd say it has something to do with a certain gentleman."

Millie covered her face with her hands. She knew that

at some point her friends would realize she and Reid were dating for real. That was supposed to come out at Hazel and Thomas's wedding where the attention would be on Hazel. Not here, sitting in a booth where she was held hostage by a tall stack of chocolate chip pancakes.

Her pink ears gave her away.

"You're kidding," Steph said. Her mouth gaped open. "Please tell me you didn't fall for Reid's charms."

That was a low blow. Millie looked at her friend, unsure how she was supposed to answer. Reid had taken both Dawn and Steph out. He had ghosted both of them. They were in their rights to be suspicious, but this was also Reid they were talking about. The guy who jumped in to help whenever Millie needed it. The guy who hung out as a chaperone for high school students because he knew it was important to her.

"He's not who you think he is," Millie said.

"Oh, honey." Dawn reached out to cover her hand. "I thought the same thing. Steph had warned me about the guy, but I didn't listen either. I mean, you've seen his face. A woman wants to give a gorgeous face like that a chance."

The walls were closing in. Everything Dawn was saying was valid, and yet her friends were so far from the truth, it was comical. The only part Dawn got right was how handsome Reid was.

"I don't know what to tell you guys except this." Millie placed her fork down and crossed her hands. "Reid is different. He's attentive and sweet. He respects my job, and he respects my time. You know how sometimes when you're dating someone, there's the little voice in the back of your head warning you to be careful?"

The women nodded. "Yeah. I know that voice." Steph looked out the window. "It's been talking to me ever since I started dating Reggie. We're probably going to break up soon."

Hazel gave Steph a hug.

Steph looked straight at Millie. "I obviously don't know all the answers to dating since my love life is a complete train wreck. I'm worried about you though. You might want to end things before you get too far in."

Millie reached for Steph's hand. "I'm sorry that things are falling apart for you, Steph. The thing is, I don't have that voice in my head when I'm with Reid. In fact, the more time I spend with him, the crazier I am about him. I count the minutes until I can see him again. He isn't like any other guy I've dated."

Dawn was resting her chin on her hand, a dreamy look in her eyes. "You're describing what I want."

Hazel grinned. "You're describing what I have with Thomas."

Steph snorted. "Have I landed in la la land? You're talking about Reid Matthews, right? Do I need to hand you a list of the women he's hurt?"

"That's not fair," Dawn said.

Millie pressed her hand against her knee to stop it from bouncing. "It's okay, Dawn." She turned her attention to Steph. "I appreciate you looking out for me. I really do. But I'm a big girl. I can make my own decisions. Besides, he makes me happy. Don't you want me to be happy?"

Steph crossed her arms and looked out the window. She ran a hand through her hair before turning back. "Of course. I always want you to be happy. That's why I'm worried."

Hazel reached for the syrup. "If it's any consolation, I've seen the way Reid acts around Millie. It's rare to see a guy that's as smitten as he is."

"Alright." Steph reached for her fork. "I'll try to give him the benefit of the doubt."

The conversation moved to other topics, but Millie couldn't shake Steph's words. Was she making a huge mistake in trusting Reid? He was ticking every box on her list, but was it possible she was too close to the situation to see clearly?

She had gone to breakfast to enjoy time with friends, but she was leaving with doubt in her heart. It wasn't how she wanted to feel heading into the week.

With school out for the summer, Millie was finally able to spend time on her projects. She had started painting a set of snowmen for her front porch last year. Like most of her hobbies, she had underestimated the amount of time it would really take. When December rolled around, her porch had been bare.

This year was going to be different. Millie was going to finish each project or give away the supplies. She mentally needed her house to be cleared out.

Millie was applying a coat of white paint to one of the

snowmen's bodies when her doorbell rang. "I'm coming," she said. She opened the door to find Reid standing on her porch, a bouquet of flowers in his hand.

"Oh no. Did I forget about a date?" Millie rubbed her nose and Reid began to laugh.

"No. I just wanted to stop by and say hi, but it looks like you're a little busy." He stretched his hand out and wiped the tip of her nose, holding up a finger dotted with white. "What are you painting?"

Millie glanced down at her hands where the white paint clearly wasn't dried yet. "Other than myself? I'm finishing one of my Christmas projects."

"I see. Isn't it a little early for Christmas?" Reid held the flowers out.

Millie buried her face in the petals, inhaling the scent of the roses. "It's actually late. If I had been on top of things, this project would have been done last year."

"Got it." Reid glanced at his phone. "I was on my way home, but I don't need to be there yet. Can I help?"

"You want to help me paint?" Millie pulled him close and kissed his cheek. "I'd love that." She led the way to the kitchen and handed Reid a paintbrush before arranging the flowers in a vase.

"Anything I need to know?" Reid was staring at the snowman like it was going to bite him.

"I'd say to stay between the lines but there aren't any. Maybe keep the paint smooth so I don't have any huge streaks."

"Yes, boss."

Millie watched Reid carefully dip his brush into the white paint, picking up the smallest dollop of paint possible. His brow furrowed with concentration while he tried to keep his hand steady. At the rate he was going, it would be fall before he finished one side.

"How is Thomas doing?" Millie feathered the top of her snowman to smooth out the edges. "Is he as unbearable as Hazel is getting to be?"

Reid rolled his eyes. "The guy needs to relax. He's been more amped up this week than I've seen him in months."

"He isn't getting cold feet, is he?" Millie didn't want her best friend to get hurt.

"Just the opposite. He complains every day about why they were waiting so long to get married." Reid turned the snowman over in his hand, trying to get every angle.

"I love that he thinks a three-month engagement is too long." Millie had gasped when Hazel told her their timeline, but it made sense. Thomas and Hazel had been friends for years. They didn't need to get to know much more about each other.

You should date someone for every season before you get married. It was the advice her mom gave her when she was heading off to school.

At the time, Millie had brushed it off as the advice of an overprotective mom. Now Millie could see the wisdom in it. That was how she planned to proceed when she got serious with a guy.

A small flutter started in her stomach. She always talked about dating someone as something she'd do in the future, but now she was starting down that path with Reid. The flutters intensified. Was he the guy she'd end up with forever? The idea was intimidating, but not scary.

Reid held the snowman out in front of him to study it, turning it from side to side. "Porter told him repeatedly to slow down, but Thomas is going to do what Thomas wants. He's always had a stubborn streak."

Reid turned the snowman towards Millie for her inspection. She held back a laugh. There were blobs of white on the bottom half and almost no white at the top of the snowman's head. It was time to give the cowboy an easier task.

"How about you finish this guy?" She handed over the snowman she had been working on. The base layer was already in place. All Reid had to do was re-paint the spot where her fingers had been holding the snowman.

"You know, I still don't understand why either of my brothers are in such a hurry to get married. What is the point?"

Millie snapped her eyes to Reid's. "Don't you plan to get married?"

"Eventually." Reid dipped his brush in a cup of water, swirling it to get it clean. "I mean, if I met the right woman and the timing was right, I'd consider it."

"I see." Millie grabbed the cup of paint water and headed to the sink. She poured the water down the drain, watching it swirl in a circle before it drained away. Steph and Dawn's words from the diner echoed through her mind. They had warned her to stay away from Reid. They said he was a player and that he hadn't changed. Why hadn't she believed them?

Her eyes were moist when she turned to look at Reid and she knew her answer. She hadn't believed them because their words just didn't make sense. The guy sitting at the table was saying all the wrong things, but he was there doing a silly painting project because he wanted to spend time with her. How was she supposed to interpret that?

It was time to invest in a good pair of ear plugs and ignore her friends. Until Reid proved himself to be a bad guy, she was going to trust their relationship. He was casually saying he didn't want to get married, but neither did she. At least, not for a while.

The newspaper on the table crinkled when Millie sat back down. "Do you want to paint one of the faces?"

The look Reid gave her had her cracking up.

"Only if you want me to mess them up." Reid held out his paintbrush. "I'm finally getting the hang of the white paint. Let's not get too crazy."

"Alright, cowboy. I'll let you stick to the ranching, and I'll do the fancy stuff."

"Good idea." Reid reached for the white tube and squirted another dollop onto his paper plate. He tapped his chin, studying the different sized snowmen on the table and reached for the smallest one. "Did I ever tell you about the time we tried to surprise my parents by decorating a tree?"

"Why do I feel like this is going to have a bad ending?"

Reid laughed. "Probably because we were always

getting into mischief. Most of my best childhood stories have a bad ending. This time, it was Hope's idea."

Millie settled in for story time while she worked. By the time the project was finished, night had fallen. In the end, she had convinced Reid to try to paint a couple of the snowmen's faces. The crooked carrot noses added to the snowmen's charm.

In the winter, Millie would proudly display her decorations on her front porch. Every time she passed them, she'd be reminded of her day with Reid. Instead of feeling happy, melancholy settled over Millie's heart.

She wanted to experience the winter months with Reid. She wanted to be in his arms when the snow began to fall. She could picture him laughing as he wrapped a scarf around her neck. There would be hot cocoa toasts and long nights snuggling under warm blankets while she made him watch every romantic movie she could find.

Millie was ready to move past the spring and summer seasons of dating. She wasn't ready for marriage, but she yearned for a relationship that would last through the year, seeing all the changes that the seasons brought.

Sleep didn't come easily for Millie that night. She was ready to give her heart to Reid, but she was beginning to think he'd hand it back when he was done playing. They weren't fake dating anymore, so why did the relationship still feel like it had a timeline attached to it?

The wedding was coming, and after that, she guessed Reid would walk away. The player had already spent far more time in the relationship than anyone expected. Was it wrong of her to want more?

There wasn't an easy answer to her questions. Millie pulled her covers over her head with a grunt. She was going to have to dig deep if she was going to be able to keep her walls down long enough to truly let him in. Most guys weren't worth it, but Reid was. She was all in, even if he broke her heart in the end.

CHAPTER 17

The foyer of the wedding center was buzzing with excitement, but upstairs in the men's dressing room, there was a quiet hush. Reid stood in front of a full-length mirror, smoothing down the front of his white dress shirt. In what felt like the blink of an eye, his brother Thomas was finally getting to tie the knot.

A pink silk tie hung from one of the hooks. Reid draped it around his neck, carefully tying it into a smooth knot. He tucked the narrow end of the tail into the loop on the back, a smile dancing on his lips. He hadn't anticipated what was coming when he stood in the dress shop two months ago, getting paired up with Millie. At the time, Reid was willing to do anything for his brother, including having to work with the bossy teacher who had no sense of humor.

Now he couldn't picture his life without Millie in it. In less than an hour, he was going to be escorting her down the aisle to the front of the chapel where they would be witnesses to Thomas and Hazel's union.

Reid's heart raced just thinking about it.

The door opened and Porter popped his head in. "You're the first one here? Where's the rest of the guys?"

Reid shrugged. "I saw Hudson earlier. His phone rang and he took off, but he's dressed."

"And the twins?" Porter pointed to the two ties still hanging from their hooks. "If they make the wedding start late, I'm pretty sure Thomas will string them up by their ankles."

Reid clasped his brother's arm. Porter was taking his duties as best man very seriously. "I'll find the twins, Port. You finish getting ready."

He grabbed his cobalt blue suit jacket, slinging it over his shoulder while he walked down the spiral staircase, heading for the outside patio. His hand was on the door-knob when Millie called out to him to wait. Reid turned and lifted a hand to his mouth, trying to process what he was seeing.

Millie was a vision of beauty, walking down the stairs gracefully as if she always wore floor length gowns. Her pink dress matched his tie, but he wasn't sure he deserved to stand next to such an incredible woman. Millie wasn't his equal. She was better than him in every way.

"I'm coming," Millie called. She scooped up the edge of her dress and hurried towards Reid. When she reached him, her cheeks were flushed. "Hi there, handsome."

She spun in a slow circle, her dress fanning out around her feet. Millie's dark hair was twisted in curls before it swept into a bun. Small white pearls accented the look. "What do you think?"

"I'd say you look stunning, but that would be a lie." Reid's voice caught in his throat.

Millie raised her eyebrows. "Oh, really?"

Reid reached for her hand and gave it a gentle kiss. "I'm pretty sure that all the greatest poets in the world would struggle to capture how beautiful you look. Are you sure you can handle hanging out with a regular guy like me today?"

Millie's eyes were sparkling. "I'll try my best. Where are you headed? It looks like you're trying to flee the scene."

Reid held his arm out, feeling proud when Millie put her hand in the crook of his elbow. "I am so happy you get to be my date today. I would never flee the scene without taking you with me." He pushed the door open and led her outside. "It's Finn and Wyatt. I'm supposed to be wrangling them into the dressing room."

There was a loud splash, followed by a roar of laughter coming from behind a row of tall bushes.

"What are the odds that your brothers were behind that splash?" Millie gave his arm a squeeze.

"Knowing the twins, I'd say pretty high." He followed the sound of laughter, carefully leading Millie down the center of the path so her dress wouldn't get ruined.

They followed the path through a tall hedge maze, weaving their way past carefully manicured bushes until they reached the center. The path opened into a beautiful rose garden with a marble fountain in the middle of the clearing. The prominent feature was a statue of a woman pouring water from a marble jug. As the water cascaded down, it split into different streams before falling to the water below.

Finn and Wyatt crouched near the base, their sleeves rolled up. Finn was holding the back of Wyatt's pants while Wyatt dipped his hand in the water.

"Is there money in the fountain? I thought your family had plenty to send these guys to school." Millie was whispering, but somehow Finn heard.

He jerked his chin towards Reid. "Hey, big bro. What's up?"

Wyatt teetered forward, almost falling into the pond before he caught his balance.

"Oh, hey, Reid. Want to help us?"

Reid's stomach sank. "You guys do know that your brother is getting married in less than an hour, right?"

Wyatt shook his head. "You mean two hours." He tapped the watch his grandfather gave him when he turned ten. Each of the kids in the family had been given a watch, but Wyatt was the only one who still wore his.

Finn looked at his brother. "Oh, crap. Did your watch battery die again?" He pulled his cell phone out of his pocket and turned it towards Wyatt. "Thomas is going to kill us."

"If you hurry, you will be able to sneak in without Thomas seeing you. He won't have any reason to kill you." Reid let out a sigh of relief. The boys still had plenty of time to get changed.

"What were you guys doing, anyway?" Millie asked.

Reid's stomach turned to bricks. Of course the school

teacher would want to know what mischief the boys were getting into. But that meant that they'd launch into a detailed explanation that they didn't have time for today.

The damage was done. "It's really cool," Finn said. "I've been studying ways to divert water more efficiently on the ranch. Watch this."

Millie grabbed Reid's hand and pulled him forward until they were standing next to the edge of the fountain.

Finn scooped up a rock from the base of the pool. He handed it to Wyatt and then grabbed the back of his brother's pants to steady him. Wyatt stretched across the pool of water, reaching for the base of the sculpture. He was sliding the rock into place when there was a loud tear.

The world seemed to slow down as Wyatt fell face forward into the fountain, sending an arc of water that splashed towards Millie and Reid, soaking the front of Millie's dress and Reid's suit.

Millie gasped, holding out her skirt. "Oh, that's cold." She looked down, her face falling. "My dress. The wedding. What am I supposed to do?"

The front of her skirt was completely drenched. Reid didn't know much about weddings, but he was certain that a soggy bridesmaid dress would make Millie stand out in a bad way.

The twins had mirrored expressions of horror on their faces. "Sorry," they said in unison.

"You are lucky that I'm the brother who came looking for you and not Porter. Get Wyatt to the dressing room. You'd better pray that Thomas doesn't see you on the way there."

Finn nodded and took off, leading his dripping brother towards the house.

Reid turned his attention to Millie. "Are you okay?"

Her nose was scrunched, like she was trying to hold back tears, but she was losing the battle. The legs of Reid's pants were dripping, but he had a handkerchief in his pocket that was dry. He handed it to Millie so she could dab her eyes without ruining her makeup.

"I might be in a little bit of shock, but I'm fine. Do you think Wyatt got hurt?"

Reid snorted. "Serves him right if he did. My brothers are idiots. None of this would have happened if they had gotten ready like they were supposed to."

Millie held her dress away from her body so the layers of wet fabric wouldn't drag on the ground. "All I wanted was to make sure everything was perfect for Hazel's special day. If she sees me like this, she's going to worry. I don't know what to do."

There was no easy answer. If they had more time, Millie would be able to dry out in the sun. With the ceremony starting in less than an hour, it just wasn't going to work. Reid looked at the woman beside him, his heart filling with equal parts remorse and gratitude.

She was standing, sopping wet, in the middle of a rose garden, moments away from being part of her best friend's wedding, and she wasn't falling apart. He couldn't think of another woman who would be so calm in the same situation.

Reid pulled her in for a hug, careful to not smash her hair. "We can fix this." He looked around the rose garden for inspiration, but nothing was coming to mind. Then he remembered the small bathroom he had ducked into when he arrived.

"I've got a plan," Reid said. He took Millie's hand and led her back through the maze, taking a sharp right turn when they came out. "If we're lucky, we can sneak by without anyone seeing us."

Guests were milling around the patio, cheerfully greeting one another. Reid spotted his mom near the door and made a detour to duck behind the bushes until she moved. He straightened up and took the last few steps to the bathroom, opening the door.

"That's the women's room," Millie hissed.

"Is anyone in here?" he called. There was no response. Reid turned to face Millie. "There was an air dryer in the men's restroom. I assume there's going to be one on the women's side, too. Would that work for drying out your dress?"

"Maybe, but someone might come in." Millie looked over her shoulder. "The only way this will work is if I take my dress off completely, and I'm not about to strip down in a public restroom, even for Hazel."

Reid had anticipated that response. "I'll stand guard. No one will come into this bathroom until you tell me you're ready."

There really weren't a lot of options. They had forty minutes until the ceremony started. Reid might be standing next to his brother in wet clothing, but the blue suit wouldn't show it. The important thing was getting Millie back to normal.

She shrugged, holding her hands out. "It's worth a try. You promise no one will come in?"

"I pinky promise." That was an ironclad commitment in the Matthews family.

There was a mischievous smirk on Millie's face when she stood on her tiptoes to kiss his cheek. "No peeking, sir."

"I wouldn't dream of it." Reid held the door open for Millie, letting it swing shut behind her before he leaned his back against it. If someone came by, they'd think he was trapping her in. After just a minute the door pushed against his back. He stepped forward and Millie poked her head out.

"This is incredibly awkward, but I got the zipper stuck." She turned her back to him, and Reid's heart leapt into his throat. The zipper had only gone down a couple of inches before it had gotten stuck.

"I see the problem," he said. He teased the zipper back and forth, trying to free the little slip of fabric that had gotten wedged between the teeth.

His mouth was dry while he worked. Reid hadn't ever helped to undress a woman. He was waiting until marriage for that. He hummed as he worked, trying to keep his mind on safer topics, like how many round bales of hay they'd get from the next harvest. He didn't need to study the curve of her neck or think about how nice it would be to press a couple kisses there for good luck.

When the zipper was free, Reid dropped his hands to his side. He cleared his throat a few times. "You've got the rest, right?"

Millie's blush shot to the tips of her ears. "I'm good.

Thanks." She ducked back inside and soon the dull roar of the hand dryer rumbled through the door.

Reid realized he should have gotten some paper towels from the men's room before he started his guard duty. His pants were sticking uncomfortably to his legs. He was leaning over to brush a leaf off his knee when Porter came around the corner.

"What's up?" Porter asked. "Is everything okay?"

"Yep. Why do you ask?" Reid pressed his back against the door and crossed one ankle over the other, trying to act cool.

"Um, maybe because you're blocking the women's restroom." Porter lifted an eyebrow. "Anything you want to tell me?"

Reid shook his head. "There was a little accident with a water fountain and Millie's dress. We've got it under control."

"Let me guess. Were the twins involved by any chance?" Porter ran a hand down his shirt. "I saw a rather drippy Wyatt heading to the dressing room."

Emily came around the corner, wearing a flowing purple dress that looked fairly similar to the one Millie was wearing. "Is Millie okay?" She stepped to Porter's side, grinning when he slid his hand to her waist.

They were going to attract attention if Porter and Emily didn't move on. "She's fine. She's just drenched. I'm standing guard so she can use the hand dryer to take care of her dress without being interrupted."

Emily's hand flew to her mouth. "Let me help her."

Reid shook his head. "I told her I'd guard the door. She's

currently indecent." His cheeks flushed at the thought of it.

"What if I call to her? If you open the door an inch, she'll be able to hear me over the dryer. No one will be able to see her." Emily put her hands on her hips, fixing a glare on Reid.

"But I pinky promised." Reid was going to stand his ground, no matter how stern Emily looked.

The sound of the dryer stopped, and Emily chose that moment to yell. "Millie. It's Emily. Are you okay?"

"I'm okay." Millie's voice was muffled through the door. "Reid, let her in."

Reid stepped back from the door, letting it open just enough for Emily to slip through. He wasn't sure what Emily would be able to do, but he was happy someone was helping.

Porter clamped his hand down on Reid's shoulder. "I'm guessing we'll be here for a minute. Do you want to tell me what happened?"

Reid glanced at his watch. They had a half hour until they were supposed to be lining up. "I'd love to fill you in, but can I get you to do me a huge favor?"

"What do you need?"

"Millie wasn't the only one who got soaked. I'd like to try to dry out a bit before the wedding starts."

Porter shook his head and stepped to the center between the two doors. "I'll try to guard both of you."

Reid nodded. "It's okay. Keep Millie safe. I'm not worried about being caught."

His brother laughed. "You got it. Get going. We're on the clock."

Fifteen minutes later, Reid felt like a new man. His pants were mostly dried out. Thankfully the water had missed his shoes. He wouldn't have to spend the evening in wet socks.

Porter looked up when Reid stepped out. "Now do you want to tell me the story?"

Reid jerked his head towards the door. "Are they still in there?"

"Yep. If they take much longer, we're going to have to figure out a way to stall the wedding." Porter was fiddling with the cuff of his suit jacket.

"That won't be necessary." Emily pushed the door open, holding it open for Millie.

Millie looked shy when she glanced at Reid. He held his arms open, and she stepped close, tucking her cheek against his chest. "Fingers crossed that that is the only mishap of the day," she murmured.

"Agreed." Reid could feel his heart slowing back to normal. He gave his brother a high five and together the couples headed towards the back of the processional hall.

Thomas was waiting to greet them. He rocked back and forth on his heels, cracking his neck from side to side. "Where have you guys been?"

Reid pressed his hand to Thomas's shoulder. "We were making sure everything was perfect for your special day. Are you ready for this?"

The smile on Thomas's face said it all. "I'm the luckiest man in the world."

There was no doubt that Thomas was smitten, but glancing over at Millie, Reid doubted his brother's words. With Millie at his side, Reid felt like the luckiest one in the room.

A hush fell over the room as the wedding planner cleared her throat. "I'd like to thank everyone for coming and helping to make Thomas and Hazel's day one they won't forget. If you're ready, Thomas, it's time to get started."

Thomas looked at his mom, who was standing in the back near a beautiful partition. "Is Hazel ready?"

Mom Matthews ducked her head behind the partition before straightening up. "She's ready." She walked up to Thomas's side, taking his arm. "I'm so proud of you." Her eyes filled with tears. "I know your dad would be proud too."

Thomas patted his mom's hand. "I'm sure he's here today, watching us from above."

She wiped her cheek and took a breath. "He wouldn't miss it."

The wedding planner cleared her throat once again. "If I can have each of you line up, it's go time. Thomas, you and your mom are going to head out first. Escort her to her seat like we talked about, and then take your place to the right of the pastor."

Reid's palms began to sweat. He'd been to his fair share of weddings, but this one was personal. His brother was about to make a forever commitment.

"Where's my maid of honor and best man?"

Porter and Emily lined up behind Thomas. Reid knew

what was coming. He looked over his shoulder to see Millie popping out from behind the partition. She hurried to his side, giving his hand a gentle squeeze.

"Hazel looks incredible," she whispered.

Reid was sure she did, but he knew Millie was the most beautiful woman in the room.

Dawn and Hudson lined up behind Reid, with the other bridesmaids and groomsmen filling the spaces behind them.

Strains of Pachelbel's Canon in D floated through the air. Thomas turned to look at the people in the room. "I love all of you," he said. Then he straightened his shoulders and walked through the doors to the aisle outside.

It didn't take long until Reid and Millie were heading towards the gazebo where Thomas was waiting. Delicate roses trailed down the ivy-covered trellis, with soft cream ribbons woven throughout.

Reid kissed Millie's cheek before he released her hand and let her go to the bride's side. He took his spot next to Porter, hardly able to believe that their brother was taking such a big step.

The string quartet finished their song and started to play the wedding march. All the eyes in the room turned to the back of the room where Hazel was standing, her parents on either side of her. As one, the audience rose. A hush fell over the crowd when Hazel began to walk towards her future.

Reid snuck a glance at Thomas. His brother's eyes were shining with tears while he watched his bride approach.

There was no doubt that in that moment, Thomas was truly the happiest he had ever been.

The pastor asked everyone to please be seated. Hazel handed her bouquet to Emily and took Thomas's hands. As the pastor spoke about love and commitment, Reid met Millie's eyes. He wasn't ready for that kind of commitment yet, but looking at Millie, his pulse quickened.

She winked at him, forming her hands into a small heart before she turned her attention back to the ceremony. Reid knew that whatever the rest of the day brought, he'd tackle it with Millie by his side.

CHAPTER 18

Millie was pretty sure that someone diabolical had invented the idea of wedding photos. She was on her fifth pose of awkwardly smiling at the newlyweds, her hip jutted back at an uncomfortable angle that would ensure she looked her best on camera. It was understandable that the couple would want a few good pictures, but it wasn't like the bridesmaid photos were going to be blown up full sized and put on a wall.

The wedding photographer was asking the women to stand in yet another strange pose when Reid walked behind the photographer. He pulled his hands up like a ballerina, spinning in a circle before he straightened his suit and walked off. Millie busted up laughing. At least she had come with someone who had a sense of humor.

Millie was pretty sure they had gone through every bridesmaid configuration that existed, from pretending to laugh while they fixed Hazel's veil to actually laughing when they pressed their faces close together. She thought the pictures were over but then the photographer pulled in the groomsmen and a new round of torture began.

Things got significantly better with Reid by her side. When the photographer told them to pretend like they liked each other, Reid had given her a little back massage while looking deeply into her eyes. And when Thomas and Hazel were taking photos with their parents, Reid had snuck in a quick kiss.

Apart from the fiasco with her dress, Millie thought the day was perfect. Hazel was the most beautiful of brides, from her intricately curled hair to the gauze dress that wrapped her in an ethereal cloud of white. The veil that had been trampled by the chickens was now repaired and cascading down Hazel's back. The most beautiful part was her smile. She beamed every time she looked at Thomas.

The photographer released the wedding party, holding the bride and groom back. After letting out a relieved sigh, Reid pulled her to the side. "Follow me."

He led her through a small gate that opened to the parking lot. As soon as the gate clicked shut behind them, Reid took Millie in his arms and kissed her. "I've been wanting to do that all day," he said. "Now I don't have to worry about messing up your lipstick, right?"

Flutters raced through her body, from the top of her head to the tips of her painted toenails. "I've been wanting to do that all day, too. This is an interesting choice for a secret kiss." Millie gestured to the cars. "The gardens have a much prettier view."

Voices were approaching, with the sound of laughter filling the air.

"We found something the twins can actually do to stay entertained." Reid opened the gate and the rest of the wedding party filed through holding plastic grocery bags. Millie grinned when she realized what was going on.

"Their car? Did you guys really bring stuff to decorate their car?"

Reid pointed to Porter. "You want to fill her in, Port?"

Porter nodded. "I think, as best man, it is my duty to shout it to the world that my little brother got married today."

Emily held out an armful of streamers. "And as Hazel's future sister, I have to agree."

Reid grabbed a package of balloons off the top of the decorations, tearing it open with a grin. "Let's send them off in style."

Before long, the air was filled with muffled giggles while the wedding party blew up balloons and stuffed them inside the car. Towards the end, it became a game to see who could slip just one more balloon through the barely open doors. The balloons were going to cascade out as soon as anyone tried to get in.

Once the car was filled, they pulled out the chalk markers.

Reid held a pink one out to Millie. "I've seen your handwriting. Do you want to do the honors?" He pushed a giant bow to the side while Millie scrawled a message across the front window.

Mr. & Mrs.

Together forever

Millie's heart was filled with happiness for her friend. Hazel had found her forever person and she was ready for her new phase of life.

On the back window Millie drew a giant heart. She wrote another message in the middle. *And they lived happily ever after.*

Millie held out the marker. "Who wants to sign our work?"

Bree grabbed the marker. "I'm not shy." She scrawled her name on one of the windows.

Emily held her hand out. "My turn." She signed her name across the top of the driver's side window. Porter stepped up beside her, drawing a heart and then his name.

"Aw, Emily hearts Porter. That is adorable." Bree gave her brother a good-natured jab in his ribs.

Steph drew a flower with her initials in it.

As the wedding party worked, Millie reached for Reid's hand. They stepped back so there was more room for people to sign their names. "Everyone is having fun. Do you think the couple will like it?"

Reid shook his head. "Thomas will hate it, but I think he'll laugh. What about Hazel?"

"We warned her not to park in an obvious place. She didn't listen."

"Heads up," Dawn called.

A roll of streamers was flying towards them. Reid caught it and handed it to Millie. "I think that's our cue to get back to work."

By the time the wedding party was finished, every inch

of the car was covered in streamers. There were tin cans attached to strings that hung under the car, ready to rattle as soon as the couple started driving.

"It's like a party cake," Bree said. "All they can see is the frosting, but they will discover more layers as the car is unwrapped."

"Thanks, crew." Porter picked up a balloon that had fallen to the ground and nestled it next to the bow. "You did good." He grabbed the loose plastic wrappings, filling up the now empty bags with trash.

Millie straightened her dress. "I guess we'd better get back to the party. Their couple photos are going to be done soon, and I don't want Hazel to get suspicious."

"Good point." Reid held Millie's hand while they headed towards the gate.

As the evening wore on, Millie watched how Reid interacted with his siblings. He swung his sisters around the dance floor, laughing as people cleared the way for them. Every time Reid passed his mom he stopped to check if she needed anything. All his interactions with his brothers felt natural, except for when he passed Hudson.

Their strained relationship was so subtle, it took Millie a while to pick up on it. While the rest of the brothers would jab each other in the ribs or give a good-natured punch on the shoulder, they all were more reserved around Hudson.

Millie made a point of watching Hudson at various points through the event. When Porter made his best man's toast, Hudson's glass was barely raised. The groomsmen surrounded Thomas, carrying him to the dance floor but Hudson hung behind. It wasn't just the way he acted around Reid. He was reserved around everyone.

The reception was in full swing when Hudson disappeared completely. Millie didn't want to interfere in Matthews family business, but her friend had been paired with him. Dawn looked lonely, sitting on the sidelines while everyone else danced.

Millie pulled Reid from the dance floor, heading to an alcove that was a little quieter. "Is there something going on with Hudson?"

Reid shrugged. "Why do you ask?"

"I know it's probably none of my business, but he keeps ditching Dawn."

"They didn't really know each other before this event, did they?" Reid pushed his hair back. "Did you think they'd get together?"

Millie rolled her eyes. "Definitely not. But I thought I'd see him hanging out with the wedding party more than he has been. He seems like he doesn't want to be here."

She sat quietly, waiting for Reid to answer. He cupped his hand to the back of his neck before stretching it from side to side. "Honestly, until we saw him last night, we weren't sure he was going to come."

Millie could read the discomfort in Reid's eyes. She rubbed his knee, trying to lend support. "We don't have to talk about it if you don't want to. There's still a party happening in the other room. Let's go dance."

Reid trailed his finger along Millie's hand. "It's not that I don't want to talk about it. I'm honestly just not sure how to." He leaned back against the cream cushions, crossing his foot over his knee.

"I think it all started when my dad passed away. You know he was in an accident at the rodeo, right?"

Millie nodded. "I know he was thrown from his horse, and he landed wrong."

"The doctors say it was a one in a million chance that he'd land how he did. For me and my older brothers, watching our dad die made it easy to walk away from the rodeo. We weren't going to make our mom bury a child alongside her husband."

Losing a parent wasn't something Millie had ever experienced. She had buried her grandma when she was fifteen, but that was it. Her heart ached for how Mom Matthews and the rest of the family must have felt.

"I'm guessing Hudson didn't feel the same?" Millie leaned into Reid's side, knowing he would wrap his arm around her and hold her close.

"The rodeo is something he and my dad did together. They rode and trained together almost every day. I was too caught up in my own grief at the time to realize that Hudson didn't just lose a dad. He lost someone who shared his dreams. When we all walked away from the rodeo circuit, he felt abandoned."

Reid fell silent. His arm around Millie was comforting to her, but she wished there was more she could do. How did you help a family that had been slowly splintering apart over the years?

"Is that why Hudson moved away?" Millie figured she already knew the answer.

The cushions shifted beneath Millie as Reid adjusted his seat. "I wish I could say that I handled things better back then, but I can't. There were some harsh words exchanged and we were young. I was only twenty-three, but I thought I had all of life's answers figured out. I was wrong."

"So, Hudson feels like an outcast. You guys acted awkward around him years ago, and no one tried to mend the relationship. Now he feels even more alienated. Does that sum it up?"

"I mean, yes. If you put it bluntly." Reid folded his arms.

"I don't mean to sound harsh, but honestly, I just don't get it. Where does the forgiveness piece come in?" Millie waved towards the room where the wedding festivities were happening. "Your dad died seven years ago. There is no denying that that was a tragedy. But is this how he'd want to see his family now? I'm sure he would have done anything for you guys when he was alive. What will it take to bring the family back together?"

Millie was stepping into territory that she had no right to be in. She gave Reid's arm a gentle squeeze. "I'm sorry. It's not my place to say anything. I'm just tired of seeing people getting hurt when all they had to do was have an honest conversation. I can't tell you the number of students I've watched get hurt over the years because the adults in their lives don't care enough to work through the difficult times."

Reid stood up from the alcove. "You're right. It isn't really your business." He ran his hand down the front of his suit. "You're also the first person in a long time who has taken the time to care. That means something to me."

Millie's heart was racing when Reid pulled her to her feet. He kissed her gently on each cheek, wrapping her in his arms before he kissed her lips. Her spirits soared. A lot of people would be offended that she had approached the subject, but not Reid.

"I don't know what the solution will be, but I am willing to reconcile if Hudson is."

"And if he isn't willing to reconcile?" Millie tilted her head back so she could see the gold flecks in Reid's green eyes.

"I don't know what I'll do if he is still mad, but at least I'm willing to try to make amends."

"That's the man I know and love." Millie grabbed Reid's hand and began to walk towards the crowd. She made it a step before she realized Reid wasn't following along beside her. When she turned back, Reid was trying not to laugh.

She gave his hand a gentle tug in the right direction. "What's wrong? I thought you wanted to go back in."

Reid grinned, a crooked smile that shot straight to Millie's heart. "You, uh, love me? That's kind of a big deal."

Millie dropped his hand as if it was on fire. "What are you talking about? I didn't say that."

She wasn't sure why he was choosing this moment to tease her.

"Oh, yes you did."

Millie thought back to their conversation. She had been being supportive, but she was sure she hadn't made any declarations. Then the heat flooded her face. Reid was right, but that wasn't what she meant.

"That doesn't count. I was saying a cliché phrase that everyone uses."

Reid tucked his hands in his pockets, rocking back on his heels. "I'm pretty sure I heard what I heard. I mean, I can't blame you. I'm a pretty good catch." He winked and started walking towards the reception hall.

Millie smacked him on the back. "You know you're the worst, right?"

Reid began laughing. "I'm just giving you a hard time." He stopped outside the french doors that led back to the crowded room. "Seriously, though, I'm glad you asked me about Hudson. I've let things fester for so long, I'm kind of numb to how bad things have gotten."

Millie slid her hand in his. "I have faith that you can make it better." She followed Reid inside, her nerves struggling to unknot. Saying she loved Reid was a figure of speech, and yet she couldn't deny that she was starting to develop feelings for the guy.

She had to figure out if she was ready to open her heart to love. For now, she was content to keep getting to know the man on her arm. There would be plenty of time to explore her feelings later.

They were heading towards the dessert bar when Bree ran to Millie's side. "It's time for the bouquet toss. Hazel wants all her bridesmaids in the front."

"That's my cue," Millie said. She squeezed Reid's hand and then followed Bree on a weaving path through the room, helping her to gather the women of the wedding party. A slow song was winding down as they made their way to Hazel's side.

There was a loud screech followed by someone tapping on a microphone. "Can everyone hear me?" Porter stood at the front of the room. "It's getting close to the time of night when I get to roast, I mean, toast the happy couple."

There was a spattering of laughs through the audience.

"Before I do that, we're going to take care of the bouquet and garter belt tosses. Can I get all the single ladies up to the front?"

Before long, a dozen women had joined the bridal party. They formed a loose crowd, leaving a large space between themselves and the bride. Hazel turned to look at everyone, a large smile on her face when she took her bouquet from Thomas. She winked at Millie before facing the wall.

"One." The air in the room was electric.

"Two." Everyone in the crowd was counting out loud.

"Three." There was a collective gasp as Hazel's flowers flew into the air. They made a high arc before coming down to land in Millie's open hands.

Millie was surrounded by women, congratulating her on being the next one to get married. She shook her head, holding the flowers out to Hazel. "Do you want to try again? I'm not ready for marriage any time soon."

"I wasn't either," Hazel said. She squeezed both of Millie's hands. "Sometimes love has a way of sneaking up on you."

Millie glanced at Reid, who was making a pointed effort to look away. His face was somber, missing the teasing smile that always danced on his lips. If her friends didn't stop talking soon, they were going to ruin every chance she had with the guy.

Porter's voice boomed across the room again. "Single guys. It's your turn. Line up." He scanned the crowd, calling men up who had been lingering in the back.

"All my brothers better be standing front and center," Porter said.

"That means you, too," Finn called. "You're not married yet."

Porter shook his head. "I'm engaged to my beautiful Emily. I don't need a garter belt to tell me she's the one."

The crowd grew silent as Thomas made his way to where Hazel was sitting on a wooden chair. He leaned forward to kiss her before glancing back at the group of men. There were a few catcalls as well as a handful of men giving him the thumbs up.

Thomas reached under Hazel's dress and carefully slipped a lacy white garter belt off her leg. He flung it into the air before spinning around to watch the men fight to grab it.

Millie's heart was in her throat when one hand reached past the others and snagged the belt mid-flight. The men stood back to leave a victorious Reid standing in the center of them, the garter belt clutched in his hand.

He looked at Millie, his eyes traveling to the bouquet in her hands. The entire wedding party was studying the couple, the pieces clicking into place. Of all the people in the room, what were the odds of Millie and Reid being paired together?

Reid's eyes grew wide, and he dropped the garter belt on the ground like it was on fire. "No way," he said. "I'm not letting my future be dictated by a flimsy piece of fabric."

With that, he walked out of the room, leaving a stunned Millie behind. Porter cleared his throat. "On that note, who wants cake?"

Millie was able to hold back her tears while the couple fed each other bites of cake, smearing the frosting across each other's faces. She waited to sneak away until they were standing on the dance floor, surrounded by family and friends.

Once she was safely tucked in the bathroom, she let the tears fall. In a matter of minutes, Reid had gone from an adoring boyfriend to the biggest jerk on the planet. She wiped her face, refusing to let a guy ruin Hazel's wedding. By the time she joined the crowd, her smile was firmly back in place. No one needed to know how slighted she felt. Especially not Reid.

Reid stood by a weathered barn, pulling his phone out of his pocket to see if Millie had texted him back yet. A long week had passed since Reid's awkward scene at the wedding. He had left the reception before the cake cutting, going for a walk to calm his nerves. By the time he got back, Millie was avoiding him.

She had a point. He had acted like a complete fool. How hard would it have been to take the garter belt and show a little excitement for being the winner? The truth was, Reid hadn't wanted to be standing up there in the first place. He knew how it would look if he caught the garter belt right after Millie caught the bouquet. Their relationship was too new to have people trying to marry them off.

It would have been easy to step towards the back of the men and tuck his hands in his pockets. Reid was too competitive for that. As soon as the lace was flying through the air, his instincts kicked in. He was going to win, no matter the cost. The second he grabbed the belt, he realized his mistake.

All he had needed was a little air to help clear his mind. Instead, he managed to offend the one woman who had been patient with him. Instead of enjoying a final dance with Millie, Reid was forced to stand on the sidelines while she banded together with Dawn and Steph. The women swayed together on the dance floor as a unit that Reid wasn't about to break up.

Now, every day that passed reminded him of the colossal mistake he had made. He should have never tried to date Millie for real. Their fake relationship had been working great, except for the fact that his heart had gotten involved.

His worry about dating women in general was that they would get too clingy and take all his time. Now, Reid was being the clingy one because no matter how many variations of "I'm sorry" he wrote, Millie was ignoring his texts. He had to get it together and stop checking his phone every few minutes, or he was never going to get any work done.

Reid kicked a wood panel of the barn before heading to the tractor. It was time for the second cutting of hay, which meant that Reid had way too much work to do on the ranch. He didn't need to be worrying about a woman. As he drove the tractor to the field, he tried to focus on the job at hand. He lowered the mower blade and began to cut through the tall stalks, settling into a pattern as he worked up and down each side of the field.

By the time he was finished, the ground was covered

with hay which would dry out in the sun over the next couple of days. He'd cut another pasture tomorrow. There was a certain pride that came from gathering enough hay to ensure that the animals would be taken care of through the winter months. If the year was plentiful, they'd end up with extra to share with neighbors.

Reid's heart was lighter when he climbed down from the tractor. He was a disaster when it came to dating, but he was an excellent rancher. The world could fall apart around him, but at least he'd have his hay bales ready before the weather changed.

He was pulling up to the barn when Porter found him.

"Any luck with Millie, yet?"

Reid shook his head. "I don't think I'll be hearing from her ever again."

Porter crossed his arms and rested his foot on the bottom rung of the fence. "Uh huh. And you feel good about that choice?"

Reid shook his head. "No. I hate it. But I burned that relationship down just like I do every single other relationship I touch. I publicly humiliated Millie in front of friends and family. I wouldn't want to forgive me. Why would she?"

A flock of chickens wandered by, chaotically pecking the ground as they searched for bugs. One of the chickens squawked and chased down her sister, pecking at her back feathers.

Reid watched the chaos, his emotions all over the place. He looked at his brother. "How did you do it, Port? You've managed to find not just one, but two perfect women in your life. I can barely make it to a third date."

Porter slid his hat off, setting it on one of the fence posts. "I'm wondering if you've got some ideas wrong about love."

"Like what?" Reid respected his brother. He wanted to hear what he had to say.

"For starters, I haven't found a perfect woman. I don't think she exists. I have been lucky enough to find two women that I have loved with all my heart. I married Cassidy when I was in my early twenties. I thought I had all of life figured out. And, well, you saw how that worked out."

Reid would never forget how he felt when he heard that both Cassidy and the baby had died. There were many nights where he caught Porter crying once he thought everyone else was asleep. The tragedy had devastated his brother, and yet he still managed to move forward.

"What I saw was a brother who had to shoulder way more responsibilities than most. I still don't know how you got out of bed in the days following Cassidy's death."

"It wasn't easy." Porter leaned down to pull a handful of weeds.

"But you made it through. And now, years later, you've got your Emily. You say she isn't perfect, but I've never seen two people who fit together like you guys do. You're what people call relationship goals."

Porter tossed the weeds to the side and reached for another handful. "My relationship with Emily is deeper than the one I had with Cassidy. I don't know how to explain it, except that maybe it is something that comes with maturity. Emily and I have both faced and overcome some difficult trials."

Reid knelt on the ground beside his brother, helping to pull weeds so his hands were busy. "So, pretty much she's perfect."

Porter shook his head. "Not perfect. She's just someone I know I want to go through the rest of my life with. Emily is the person I want to talk to at the end of a hard day. She's the one I want to call when something exciting happens. We're taking our time with getting married, but that's because I know when I make those vows, it will be forever I'm promising her."

There was wisdom to Porter's words, but it didn't help Reid. "Perfect or not, you've been able to find love. All I am capable of doing is throwing grenades into any relationship before it can get even a little serious. I feel like someone who has been hurt so many times, I don't trust love, except that I haven't been hurt. I won't let myself get close enough for that to happen. What is wrong with me?"

The chickens were making their way back towards the brothers. Porter threw a handful of weeds their way. "I'm not a psychologist, but I've spent enough time with Emily to know that if the problem doesn't have an easy answer, there is usually more to it beneath the surface. I can't tell you why you don't let women get close. That is for you to figure out. What I can tell you is that there is nothing wrong with you. You're a guy trying to navigate life the best way he knows how. I've seen you tackle obstacles your entire life. If you don't like how things are going, maybe it's time to take a serious look in the mirror."

Porter straightened up and reached for his hat. He rested his hand on Reid's shoulder. "For what it's worth, I thought you and Millie were good for each other. If your heart is pulling you towards her, maybe it's time to take that leap."

He headed towards the house, but Reid stayed behind, methodically clearing the rest of the weeds from the ground in front of him. He knew what he wanted. What he didn't know was how to get Millie to give him a chance.

* * *

LATER THAT AFTERNOON Reid and Porter loaded into a truck and headed over to Hazel's house. That was where Thomas and Hazel would be staying until their house on the ranch was complete. Reid was lifting a dresser out of the truck with Porter when he heard Millie's voice.

His hands were full as he helped lift the dresser out of the truck, so he wasn't able to see where she went. When he turned around, Millie was nowhere to be seen.

Reid's pulse began to race. He picked up his end of the dresser and headed towards the house, hoping that Millie would be inside. He and Porter followed Thomas to the bedroom at the end of the hall. He could hear laughter coming from the kitchen, but Reid wasn't going to drop the furniture just so he could go check if she was there.

They slid the dresser to the wall and Porter headed out

to get a box. Thomas hung back and reached for Reid's arm, pulling him to a stop in the hallway. "Millie is here."

"I know." Reid's hands were trembling at the thought of seeing her face to face again.

"You're not going to make it awkward, right?" Thomas's face was serious. "Hazel has been worried."

Reid shook his head. "It's all good, Thomas. I don't want to ruin anything for your first day home. Welcome back, by the way."

A smile beamed across Thomas's face. "I'm still trying to wrap my mind around this being our place instead of just Hazel's. I won't have to leave at the end of the day."

"You look happy." Somehow, Thomas seemed even more in love than he had been on his wedding day.

"I really am." Thomas clapped his brother on the back. "Let's get more boxes."

Reid followed his brother back down the hall, pausing to glance in the kitchen when he passed. Millie stood in a group with Hazel, Hope, Dawn, and Steph. She glanced up, meeting Reid's eyes, and his blood ran cold.

In the matter of a week, Millie's eyes had gone from warm and inviting to guarded and a little sad. She wasn't looking at him like a friend, but rather like a stranger who was threatening to steal her dog.

Reid ducked his head and continued out to the truck, filling his arms with boxes that he brought back in. He kept his head down while he worked. He had already caused a small scene at his brother's wedding. There was no way he was going to cause any more trouble at his new house.

There wasn't a lot of stuff to move. Hazel's house was

already furnished, so they had just brought the necessities for Thomas to be able to settle in. Most of the boxes contained his clothes. They would move the rest of Thomas's things to the barn house when it was finished.

Thomas and Hazel walked the brothers to their truck. "Thanks for bringing this over," Thomas said. He wrapped his arm around his wife. "We're ready to get settled in."

Reid gave them each a hug. "I'm happy for you guys. Let me know if you forgot anything and we'll bring it over."

He was climbing into his truck when Millie came out of the house. She lifted a hand to wave, and Reid had to swallow the giant lump in his throat. She wasn't coming to talk to him, but instead she headed for Hazel.

The dismissal was clear. If Millie wasn't ready to talk to him in a neutral place like his brother's new house, she wasn't going to want to talk to him anywhere. He gripped the steering wheel so tightly, his knuckles turned white.

Porter was silent for most of the drive home. "Do you want to talk about it?" he finally asked.

Reid shook his head. "There isn't anything to say. You saw how she looked at me."

"Yeah. That was rough."

"When will I learn? I had a beautiful woman who was good for me, and I blew it." Reid pulled into the driveway and shut the engine off. Instead of heading towards the house, he made his way to the horse barn. He needed to spend time with someone who wouldn't judge him for his actions.

Riding around the perimeter of the ranch gave Reid time to clear his mind. He wasn't willing to give up on

Millie yet. They both deserved a face-to-face conversation. Then, if she decided that she was really finished with Reid, he'd let her go.

An hour later, Reid was back in the stables brushing down his horse. He stopped to pat Sunflower on the nose before heading to his favorite thinking spot. Reid pulled out his phone and leaned back against the trunk that was worn from years of use. He closed his eyes and prayed that the Lord would help him know what to say. Then he sent a quick text.

Millie. I know I'm the last person you want to hear from. I'm asking you for one conversation, face to face or even on the phone. Then I promise to respect your wishes.

He sent the message and leaned back once more, putting his faith in the Lord and his trust in the woman he was crazy about.

Millie didn't respond until the evening. Her text gave Reid hope. **I agree that we need to talk in person. Can you meet me tonight?**

Definitely. Where?

Reid impatiently watched the three dots flicker across his screen, waiting for Millie's answer to come through. They started and disappeared a couple of times before the text appeared.

Let's meet at Sunny's Cafe. Does a half hour from now work?

Reid glanced down at his outfit. With driving time, he wasn't going to have long to get ready. **I'll be there.**

After the quickest shower in the world, Reid took his

time to look through his clothes for a shirt that Millie liked. He carefully combed his hair, sweeping it out of his eyes. Then he dabbed on some aftershave, patting his cheeks. If this was his last chance to see Millie, he was going to make a good impression.

He had two minutes to spare when he pulled into the parking lot. There was a group of high school students crowding near the door. They were surrounding someone while they waited to place their orders. When the students moved on, Reid could see that Millie had been the focus of their group.

She turned to scan the parking lot, and the smile that had been on her lips fell away. By the time Reid lifted his hand to wave, her wary look was back.

"Thanks for agreeing to meet me," Reid said.

Millie shrugged. "Our relationship was important to me. I thought it deserved an ending in person."

That was a blow. Millie's intentions were clear. It didn't seem to matter what Reid said. Her mind was made up.

"So, this is the end?" Reid tucked his hands in his pockets.

"You were pretty clear at the wedding." Millie wasn't holding back her words.

Reid rocked forward on his toes. "It's not like that. I mean, I guess it kind of was."

Millie's eyes were blazing. "You threw the garter belt on the ground and stormed out. If a simple wedding tradition is going to push you over the edge, I'm not sure where we really stand."

The words were landing like punches to his stomach.

Reid held his hands out. "I'd like to say there was a reason for that, but I don't have one. I panicked."

"You do realize that wasn't a binding, legal agreement, right? Catching the bouquet didn't automatically make me the next woman to get married, and catching the garter belt certainly didn't mean the same for you." Millie's hands were on her hips. Her entire body was leaning forward as the words continued to spill from her mouth.

"The stupid thing is that everyone warned me about you. They said you were someone who couldn't commit. And like a crazy person, I believed I was the exception. I thought we were in a pretty good place, but the simplest suggestion of a commitment had you running for the door. I deserve better than that."

Reid's ego was deflating faster than a balloon. He deserved every accusation she was throwing at him, and much worse. The fire in her eyes made it clear that they weren't going to be heading into the cafe any time soon. She'd rather be anywhere else.

"You're right." Reid wanted to walk away with what little dignity he had left. "I knew I was getting close to you, and I threw it away. I panicked and let my fears win."

Millie gave a curt nod. "Can you at least tell me why? What are you afraid of?"

That was the question that had been plaguing Reid since the wedding. In all his soul searching and all his praying, he still hadn't found his answer. "I don't know. I wish I had a better answer, but I really don't know what is holding me back. You are easily the best woman I've ever dated, fake or real, and I still managed to mess things up."

Reid hooked his thumbs through his belt loop and looked up towards the sky, wishing that the heavens would open, and someone would come give him the answers he so desperately wanted.

Millie stepped forward and placed her hand on his arm. He automatically wrapped his arm around her in a hug.

"I messed up and I can't take it back. What can I do?"

Millie lay her head against his chest. "I think, for now, we need a break. I need time to sort out my feelings for you and you need time to figure out what you want from life."

Her words made sense, but it didn't soften the blow. "I don't like that." Reid was standing in front of a cafe, his arms around the woman he was crazy about, and she was dumping him. He needed a way to make it better.

"Reid, I don't like it either. I wish we could go back to the way things were before the wedding, but we both know that can't happen." She stood on her tiptoes and pressed a kiss to his cheek.

Reid inhaled deeply, memorizing everything from the smell of her shampoo to the softness of her lips against his skin. He gave her a final squeeze and then he dropped his arms to his side.

Millie turned for the parking lot, taking his heart with her. In the end, it didn't matter how hard he prayed. Millie had her agency, and she was using it to protect her heart.

"Wait. Millie?" Reid's heart was thumping out of his chest when she turned. "Where does that leave us? Will I ever get to talk to you again?"

Millie hugged her arms to her chest. "How about we

start back at the beginning and see how we do as friends? We can work our way forward from there."

Reid nodded, a glimmer of light filling his heart. He may not be boyfriend material, but he was going to do his best to win back her friendship. The hard part would be figuring out how.

CHAPTER 20

Time was flying by for Millie. She had started her summer break dating a handsome cowboy. When Reid had proposed the fake dating scenario, Millie couldn't have guessed how quickly her feelings would grow. She had gone to Thomas and Hazel's wedding caught up in the romantic notion of a happily ever after.

Now, with less than two weeks to go before school started, Millie was painfully single again. Her relationship with Reid had burned bright, but their flame was extinguished before they had time to move past the kindling phase. As much as her friends tried to convince her that she was better off without Reid, he had left a hole in her life that she couldn't fill.

It had been three weeks since they agreed to try being friends, and so far, nothing had come of it. Every time Millie picked up her phone to text Reid, she put it down again. What was she supposed to say? He certainly didn't have time for idle chit chat, and neither did she.

Instead of trying to focus on what she was missing with Reid, Millie turned her attention to clearing out the rest of her craft closet. Even that was proving to be dangerous. Millie pushed a bin of ribbon to the side only to come face to face with one of the snowmen she had painted with Reid.

She pulled it out of the closet, turning it over to look at the front. Reid's hand hadn't been steady when he held the brush, resulting in a lopsided smile that he had wanted to paint over. Millie told him it was perfect.

Now, holding the snowman in front of her, Millie wondered if she had judged Reid a little too harshly for his actions at the wedding. He had messed up, but much like the snowman in front of her, he had flaws. They all did. She had no right to expect him to be perfect in every situation.

She smiled when she thought about the way Reid had stood in front of the bathroom door, promising to guard it so no one would catch her awkwardly drying her dress under a hand dryer. A flush came to her face when she remembered his help with the zipper. He could have taken advantage of her situation, unzipping her dress all the way. Instead, he was a perfect gentleman, only unzipping the section of the dress that was stuck.

That was the problem with fake dating Reid. The relationship had started on a ruse, but the man behind the contract was very real. He loved his family. He was loyal. He worked hard. He respected Millie.

More than that, he had shown her what it felt like to be held by a man who was willing to put his own needs to the side to make sure she was comfortable. Reid never pressured her to act like their relationship was more than a pretend fling, but somehow, they had both developed real feelings.

Millie grunted and reached for another box in the closet. She needed to focus on the job at hand and not the cowboy who commanded her thoughts. She sternly reminded herself that she didn't need Reid's help to lift the boxes after she filled them with donations.

It was time for a better distraction. Millie flipped on her laptop and logged in to her teacher account. Registration for the high school students had opened that morning. Millie wanted a sneak peek of who she'd be teaching.

She was scanning through the names in her creative writing class when a certain name jumped out at her. Bree Matthews. Just reading her name brought back a flood of memories. Bree had been part of Reid's earliest dating games, from passing balloons and notes to making Mr. Albertson be responsible for the student's fundraiser.

In those early days, Bree had been near Reid with every step he made. How was Millie supposed to teach his sister? Every class period she'd see Reid's features on Bree's face. Bree didn't seem like the judgmental type, but Millie wasn't sure if she'd be respectful in class. Maybe she'd start rumors about what a bad person Millie was.

Millie slammed the laptop closed, looking for a better distraction. She flipped on the tv, scrolling through her Netflix account to see what she wanted to watch next. It was a debate between a new romcom or one of her classic favorites. She was putting a bag of popcorn into the microwave when her phone buzzed.

Reid's name flashed across the screen. **I tried to patch things up with Hudson. It isn't going how I planned. Can we talk?**

Millie started to type a response, but she wasn't sure she wanted to spend the evening texting back and forth. If it was a real problem, Millie wanted to be able to hear Reid's voice. It was much easier to hear emotion in person. Pushing a small wave of panic aside, she swiped to his phone number and pushed the call button.

He answered on the second ring. "Millie. Thanks for calling. I need your advice."

The sound of Reid's voice coursed through her body. There was an emptiness in her heart that ached when she heard him say her name.

"What's going on? What happened with Hudson?" Millie wiped at the tears that were beading in her eyes. She didn't need Reid to know that she was overwhelmed being able to talk about something real with him again. So much for just being friends.

Reid's voice wavered. "I came to see him today. I wanted to show support for him in the rodeo."

"How did it go?"

"Millie, I left fifteen minutes in. The rodeo is still going, but I can't sit there. I can't watch my brother throw away his life."

Millie headed to the backyard, with Rex trailing behind her. "That's a little harsh. Why don't you start at the beginning and tell me why you're worried?"

She lay back in the hammock, letting Reid's voice wash over her as he told her about driving three hours to watch his brother compete. Millie couldn't help but feel proud of Reid. She knew, with the role the rodeo played in his past, that it hadn't been an easy decision. She closed her eyes, fighting against the urge to go to Reid and hold him while he talked.

Reid said something about bulls and Millie sat up. "Wait. Your brother is a bull rider? I thought you said he did steer wrestling."

"That's what we thought he did. Every rodeo event comes with some risk, but I didn't think he'd be stupid enough to go for the most dangerous event of all."

Millie had gone to the rodeo a couple of times growing up. The bull riding event always left her sitting on the edge of her seat. She couldn't understand how a human would volunteer to get flung around like a doll by an animal that weighed over a thousand pounds. Eight seconds in the arena was over in a blink, but the injuries carried by the bull riders left a lasting mark.

Now the harsh reaction made a little more sense. "I'm sorry, Reid. That's got to be hard." Millie's heart hurt for her friend.

"I don't know what I am supposed to do. Do I head back to the rodeo and pretend to be proud of my brother, knowing that every ride could be his last? I don't think I can do that."

Millie said a quick prayer that she'd have the right advice for Reid. She waited a beat until she could feel the Lord guiding her. "I guess it comes down to this. If Hudson got on a bull tomorrow and the worst happened, would you regret leaving today without hearing his side of things?"

Reid huffed. Millie could picture his face, his brow furrowed while he clenched and unclenched his fist. If he wasn't sitting down, he was most likely pacing around the room.

"You're right." There was the scraping of a chair against the floor. "I'll head back and try to be a supportive brother."

"You've got this." Millie's heart swelled with gratitude that he was willing to do hard things. "And Reid?"

"Yeah?"

"Hudson isn't your dad. I know your family experienced the worst loss possible but try to separate your grief about losing your dad from your fears for your brother. Hudson has a reason for doing what he's doing. Maybe hear him out and see what he has to say."

Reid cleared his throat. "Thanks, Millie. I'd better go."

He was going to hang up the phone soon. Millie had a split-second decision to make. Did she want to open the door back up for Reid to step into her life? Or did she want to close that door once and for all? Her heart knew what she needed to do.

She pressed the phone to her ear, willing her hands to stop shaking. "Let me know how it goes."

"I will." Reid's voice was low when he pulled out his pet name for her. "Bye, teacher."

"Bye, cowboy."

Millie held the phone to her chest long after Reid had

hung up. His reactions at the wedding made it very clear that he wasn't looking for anything serious, but when he had a crisis, Millie was the person he reached out to. His actions at the wedding said he wasn't interested in love, but maybe his heart was beginning to soften.

Rex hopped into the hammock, sending it swinging back and forth before he licked Millie's face with a slobbery kiss. "That's gross," she squealed before she wrapped her arms around her dog. That was when she closed her eyes and thanked the Lord for letting her talk to Reid. Hopefully something she said would help the brothers to reconcile at least a little bit.

As she pictured Reid and Hudson's reunion, a flicker of butterflies broke loose from the cocoons she had created. The flutter of possibility swirled in her stomach. Maybe her adventures with the cowboy weren't over quite yet.

It felt good to hope again.

* * *

MILLIE HAD EXPECTED that Reid would call her in the next couple of days, but her phone remained silent. She spent her time working on getting everything ready for her classes. The first day of school always brought jitters with it.

As Millie walked around the hallways of the school, she felt like something was off. She'd walk into the office, and everyone would stop talking, or try to change the subject to make it seem like they hadn't been discussing anything important. There wasn't any one thing that made Millie truly worried, but the combination of little things left her on edge.

Two days before school started, a mandatory staff meeting was called for all the teachers. Millie went to the meeting, hoping she'd finally get some answers as to why everyone had been cagy.

The vice president of the school, Mrs. Talmadge, stood to talk. She pushed her blonde hair back and straightened her shoulders. "I have some bad news for the school. Earlier this week, Mr. Albertson was removed as principal."

The entire room erupted into whispers as teachers speculated with their neighbors about what had happened. A giant pit opened in Millie's stomach. She was pretty sure she knew what had happened. Had he finally gotten caught stealing from the school?

Mrs. Talmadge held up her hand to quiet the crowd. "I'm not allowed to say too much at the time because there is a police investigation going on. What I am allowed to tell you is that the entire student budget for this coming school year is gone. No dances, no homecoming floats, no extracurricular competitions. The sports teams are going to have to work with the jerseys they have. In short, we're going to have to tighten our belts for the first month until we can get this figured out."

Millie closed her eyes, letting Mrs. Talmadge's voice flow over the top of her head. The money was gone, which meant that at one point, it had gotten tempting enough for Mr. Albertson to make a big move. She couldn't help but feel that the last fundraiser had pushed him over the edge.

"We're not asking anyone to play the blame game here," Mrs. Talmadge said. She was still talking, but Millie's mind was racing ahead to how the students would take it when their homecoming activities were canceled.

All that cash. All that work. It didn't seem possible that in one fell swoop, everything was gone. Millie sat in stunned silence while Mrs. Talmadge continued to fill the teachers in on the changes that were coming.

She glanced over at Mr. J, who had worked just as hard as she had during the fundraiser. He was slumped forward, his chin resting on his fist. It was as if he could feel the weight of Millie's eyes on him. He slowly turned, shaking his head slightly before he faced the front.

Millie had expected Mr. J to be angry at Mr. Albertson, but his accusing eyes felt very personal. Sure enough, people avoided Millie as the meeting ended and they began to file out. Millie grabbed her friend Sheila's arm and pulled her to the side.

"Why do I feel like everyone thinks this is my fault?" Millie needed her friend to tell her it was all in her mind. Sheila wouldn't meet her eyes.

"What am I missing?" Millie planted her hands on her hips. She was willing to stay in the gym for as long as it took to get Sheila to talk.

Sheila let out a big breath. "This isn't coming from me, but people say that you were the one who put the biggest temptation in front of him. When you made him count the cash boxes in front of everyone, it forced his hand. Logically, they know they shouldn't blame you, but people need somewhere to focus their anger."

The implications were insulting. "You're saying that I made him steal because I asked for accountability? That's absurd." Millie was fuming. "It shouldn't have mattered if we raised five hundred dollars or five million. If Mr. Albertson had integrity, he wouldn't have been tempted in the first place. Why aren't they blaming him?"

Sheila scuffed the tip of her shoe across the floor. "You're right, and I don't blame you at all. I'm just telling you what I've heard."

Millie nodded. She waited until everyone else left the room. Then she walked down the hallway in silence. With each step, the implications of what Mr. Albertson had done sunk in. He hadn't just taken money from the students. He had taken away their celebrations. The beginning of the school year pancake breakfast was supposed to kick things off so the students were excited to go to school. Instead, they were going to show up to somber teachers and whispers about the police and an investigation.

She started to write the first day of school greeting across the whiteboard, but her hands were shaking too much. She needed to be able to talk to someone, and clearly her colleagues weren't going to be any help. They blamed her for the situation.

Millie snapped the cap on the marker and set it on the tray. She was going to be useless until she was able to calm down. The somber mood followed her outside, where the rain was picking up.

Millie climbed into her car and buckled her seatbelt. She started the engine and backed out of her parking spot. When she reached the end of the road, she had a split decision to make. She could turn to the right and head home to snuggle with Rex and eat a bag of chocolate peanut butter cups. Or she could turn left and head somewhere where she could vent.

Millie knew that Reid was right in the middle of harvesting. She hoped the rain had given him a temporary break. The phone went to voicemail, but Millie kept driving. "Reid," she said. "I really need a friend right now. I'm heading to the ranch. Can we talk?"

As she hung up the phone, she felt the weight shifting off her shoulders. It was easier to breathe. She couldn't talk to her best friends, but she knew that whatever she told Reid would stay between the two of them. She was keeping a big secret for him. The hope was that he would be able to do the same for her.

Millie was turning on to Old Ranch Road when Reid called back.

"Sorry I missed your call. I was helping with dinner."

Millie could hear laughter in the background. She felt a pang of longing. There was something special about eating with the Matthews family. Everyone who entered the house felt loved.

Reid cleared his throat. "Do you want to join us?"

There was a strong pull to say yes, but Millie needed to vent. She certainly couldn't do that with Bree sitting across the table from her. "I wish I could, but I need to talk about things I can't share with anyone else. Something happened with Mr. Albertson."

"How close are you?"

Millie let out a small laugh. "Close. I can see the turnoff to your house."

"Give me two minutes to fill in my mom and I'll be out."

As Reid hung up, Millie turned into his driveway. Less than a minute later he was walking onto the porch. He looked towards the car and a smile beamed across his face. In that moment, Millie's troubles melted away, replaced by such a large swarm of butterflies in her stomach, she wasn't sure there was room for any other emotion.

Reid climbed into the car and turned to face her. "Are you okay?"

Millie shook her head, the tears welling up in her eyes. "Not really. Can we go somewhere private to talk?"

Reid nodded. "I know just the place." He pointed to a narrow trail that ran towards the center of the ranch.

"Are you sure my car will make it?"

The rain was starting to come down in sheets. Reid craned his head to look out the window at the sky. "It's just around the corner. I'm sure."

Millie put her trust in her cowboy and started to drive. It felt good to have a rock that she could confide in by her side.

Reid led Millie up the rickety ladder to the loft where the smaller bales of hay were stored. Before long, the entire loft would be full. For now, the hay was still drying out in the fields. It wasn't the most picturesque of settings, but no one would bother them.

"Hold on a second." Reid climbed down the ladder and ran through the rain to the storage barn next door. He opened a couple of trunks before he found what he was looking for. When he came back to Millie, he had a couple of thick wool blankets in his arms.

Millie grabbed a side, and together they spread the blankets over the ground in front of bales, making a softer spot to sit so they could talk. Reid scooted to the edge of the blanket, giving the most room to Millie. He smiled when she slid right next to his side, sitting close enough to him that he could feel the heat radiating off her body.

He tried to play it cool when Millie looked up at his face. "Is this okay? Me sitting near you? It's been a rough day." Her voice broke. "I really need a friend who won't judge me or make me feel bad for what happened."

Reid didn't answer for a minute. Instead, he wrapped his arm around her while she swiped furiously at the tears that started to fall down her face. He swayed from side to side, rocking her gently while she cried. "You can tell me anything. If anyone should be judged, it is me. I'm the one who is always managing to mess things up."

When Millie looked up again, her cheeks were splotchy, but she looked strong. She cleared her throat. "This is much worse than blurting out things you don't mean to say. You know how I was worried that Mr. Albertson was skimming money from the school?"

"Yeah." Reid had gotten a bad impression of the principal the first time he met him.

"I was right. He had been skimming off the top, but it was much worse than that."

Lead poured through Reid's veins. He had worked hard with Millie to raise money for Bree's senior year. The idea of someone taking even part of it made him furious. "What did he do? Steal part of the cash for a vacation or a car?"

Millie twirled a strand of hair that had fallen from her bun. "If that were the case, we'd have something left to work with. Reid, he completely cleared out the account."

Reid sat in stunned silence. There were checks in place so something like that couldn't happen. "I don't understand. It's not like he could just walk into the bank and withdraw the funds as the principal of the school, right?"

"Nope." Millie shook her head. "There's a police investigation going on right now. Mr. Albertson isn't talking, but best guess, he had at least one or two accomplices. However he did it, he left us in a pretty bad spot."

Fury swept through Reid. It took a special kind of low-life human to steal from kids. He could understand why Millie was upset. Something like that would demoralize the entire school.

"It gets worse." Millie's voice had never sounded so small. She looked at Reid, clasping her hands together on her lap.

"What happened?" Reid couldn't imagine anything worse than an unscrupulous principal stealing from the high school.

"Everyone blames me."

Reid had been slouching, his back against the bales. Hearing this, he jerked forward. "Who, exactly, is everyone? Do the police honestly think you were involved?"

Millie shook her head. "It's not the police. It's the rest of the staff at school. They are saying that if the last fundraiser hadn't been so good, he wouldn't have been tempted. And maybe they're partly right."

"That's absurd." Reid was struggling to keep his voice low. The last thing he needed was his family to come running because they heard him yelling. The people he wanted to yell at weren't there anyway. "Since when is it your job to make sure everyone at your school is honest?"

The tears were welling up again. "That's what I said. I know people are in shock and looking for someone to blame. I don't know why I'm the lucky one that gets to take the brunt of it. They certainly didn't have a problem with how much we raised when it was happening."

Reid was ready to drive to the school and give everyone a piece of his mind. How dare they treat Millie that way? He took a few slow breaths to calm down. "If you're at fault, I guess I am too. It was my idea to double the funds."

Millie's head snapped up, her blue eyes wide. "I didn't mean that. I'd never blame you."

"I know, I know. You shouldn't blame yourself either." If it had been a month ago, Reid would have pulled Millie onto his lap and kissed every tear away. As a friend, he wasn't sure what he was allowed to do. He settled for trailing his hand up and down her arm while he held her close, waiting for her to speak.

After a few minutes, Millie swiped her eyes and scooted to the end of the blanket. She turned so she was sitting across from him, her leg pressing against his. If Reid leaned forward, he'd be able to grab her hands. Instead, he leaned back against the bale.

"What can I do to help?" Reid picked up a piece of hay that had fallen to the ground and began to slowly peel it apart. He would march into the school and give everyone a stern talking to if he thought it would do any good, but he knew it wouldn't.

"You being here with me is enough. I needed to talk to someone who would actually listen to me without judgement."

Millie's words caressed Reid's heart. He had been working on fixing the pieces of himself that he didn't like so that when the time came, he would be ready to make that commitment. Now, with Millie sitting across from him, Reid was beginning to understand what those pieces might look like.

"Can we talk about our relationship for a minute?" Reid felt Millie's leg stiffen beside him, but then it relaxed.

"Why not? The day has already been crazy enough." Millie's voice sounded resigned, and Reid felt a pang of guilt for adding one more thing to her load. He hoped he'd be making her day better in the end.

Reid shifted his seat, wedging his back more firmly against the bales. "I've been doing a lot of thinking since the wedding. I'd say since we broke up, but I didn't even give us a chance to do that. I blew things up."

Millie nodded, but she didn't say anything. He guessed that meant she agreed.

"Here's the thing. I'm terrified of relationships, and I still don't completely know why. I think part of it is that I'm always thinking about the future. With the ranch, sometimes it feels like a game of chess. I have multiple fields to plant and harvest. If I plant too fast, there isn't going to be enough time to harvest everything before it spoils. If I don't plant enough, there might not be enough food to carry us through the winter months. I have to think about things that will happen months from now, always trying to plan a few moves ahead."

He took a breath. "Are you following?"

Millie bumped his leg with hers. "So far, I'm good. This whole ranch being a chess game analogy is a new one to me, although I don't see where our relationship fits in."

Reid ran his hand through his hair. "I'm getting to that. Or I hope I am." He took a deep breath and blew it out slowly, trying to gather his thoughts. "I'm so used to thinking forward, I often forget to slow down and pay attention to the present. When you caught the bouquet, my mind jumped our relationship to a place and time when we could be getting married. I skipped way too many steps and managed to spook myself."

"And then you caught the garter belt." Millie's words held no judgment.

"Exactly. My mind was already stressing about a future that I wasn't ready for. The garter belt seemed to cement the idea that we were going to have to get married. I no longer had a choice. And that was what broke me."

Saying the words out loud brought clarity to Reid's mind, but he felt incredibly foolish. Who threw away a relationship because they were stuck in the future?

Millie rested her arm on his leg, the pressure bringing Reid back to the present where he was sitting in a barn with the woman he cared about most in the world.

"I can understand, a little, what you are saying, but I don't know what that has to do with today." Millie studied his face, her eyes searching for answers.

"I think talking to you today is giving me a bit of clarity. No matter how hard you try to make something work, there are always going to be variables you can't control. The fundraiser is a great example of that. We put all the pieces in place to make a great year for the students. We were aware of the danger that was lurking in the corner, and we tried to prevent it. In the end, the fundraiser money got stolen and we couldn't prevent it from happening at all."

Millie's eyes were sad. Reid reached for her hand. "That wasn't either of our faults. But here's my point. If I spend all my time trying to prepare for every bad scenario that can come, I'm never going to get to live in the present. We didn't know that the money would be gone, but I know I personally had a blast working those booths. Everyone came together in the end, and that was all because of you."

Reid took another deep breath. "That leads me back to our relationship. What I'm learning is that I can't spend my time worrying about what may or may not happen in the future. Sure, we could have kept dating and a year from now, decided that we didn't want to be together. But we would have built a year filled with memories and happy moments that didn't otherwise exist."

A smile was dancing on Millie's lips.

"What are you thinking about?" Reid picked up another stalk of hay, rolling it between his fingers.

"Honestly?" Millie's cheeks pinked up. "I was thinking that you are incredibly adorable when you get fired up about something. I think I get what you are saying though."

Time slowed for Reid as he looked at the woman across from him. "So, what does that mean?"

Millie pushed up so she was kneeling in front of Reid. "I think it means that you and I have a lot to talk about. And for the first time in weeks, I think my heart is open enough to hear what you have to say."

Reid ached to close the distance between Millie and himself. Instead, he held his hand out, wrapping his fingers around Millie's hand.

"Back to the problem at hand. What can I do to help with the school?"

Millie shrugged. "Nothing really, unless you happen to have a magic wand. The kids this year are going to learn that although traditions are important, they can come together in new ways. They won't have a homecoming dance, but they can still support the football team. There won't be booster club activities that help them get to know each other, but we'll figure out ways to make the year fun. Hopefully our next fundraiser will get us back on our feet, and the rest of the year won't be a bust."

As she spoke, there was a conviction in her eyes that Reid recognized. He knew that no matter how the year went, the students were going to be fine. They had an entire school of teachers who would work hard to smooth over the disaster Mr. Albertson left behind.

Reid followed behind Millie as she climbed back down the ladder. Her head was high as she headed towards the barn door. She stopped just inside, waiting for Reid to reach her side.

"Thank you," she said. She wrapped her arms around his waist and Reid's pulse raced. "You were the friend I needed to see."

Reid hesitated for a moment before he leaned down and kissed the top of her head. "You helped me with Hudson. I'm glad I could return the favor."

Millie stepped out of his embrace and turned towards her car. "Are you ready?"

Reid nodded, and together they raced out into the rain. Reid's shoulders were soaked when he finally went back into his house, but his feet were light. For the first time since the wedding, he understood why he had pushed Millie away. Now he had hope that he could move forward and give a real relationship a try.

* * *

Keeping his mouth closed for the next two days was proving to be difficult for Reid. He knew that his little sister would be walking into a difficult first day of school, but he couldn't betray Millie's trust by spilling secrets that weren't his to share. He didn't know how the staff would end up handling the situation, but he knew nothing he did would help.

He made sure he was working near the house when Bree got home from school. She barged into the house, calling for her mom. Reid joined them in the kitchen.

Bree's eyes were bright with excitement. She was bouncing on her toes, her hands waving while she spoke. "You'll never guess what happened today."

"What happened?" Mom Matthews asked. Reid tried to look surprised even though he knew what was coming.

"Someone stole all our money." Bree turned to Reid. "You know that fundraiser we did?"

"The bake sale?" Reid was pretending to be clueless.

"That's the one. The teachers aren't telling us what happened exactly, but we're pretty sure Mr. Albertson was involved."

Mom Matthews planted her hands on her hips. "Bree. What have I taught you about gossip?"

"That it doesn't do anyone any good, and that if I hear gossip, I should let it go. But Mom, everyone is saying it. Derek's friend Felix lives on the same street as Mr. Albertson. He saw him getting put in a police car."

Reid wasn't sure how much he could share, but it sounded like the kids were figuring it out anyway.

"Anyway." Bree tossed her hair over her shoulder and grabbed an apple from the basket. "The money's gone and they took away our homecoming dance." She slumped into a chair and took a bite of the apple.

Mom Matthews looked back and forth between Bree and Reid. "That doesn't seem right. The school has all sorts of budgets in place. I'm sure they could pull from somewhere else."

Bree shrugged and took another bite of her apple. She grabbed a glass out of the cupboard and filled it with water. "I've got to call Madison and see what we're going to do." She was out of the kitchen before Reid could speak up.

Mom Matthews went to follow Bree, but Reid held her back. "She's right about everything," Reid whispered. "Millie told me all about it. Mr. Albertson is definitely guilty."

"But what about all the checks and balances that the school has in place? One man shouldn't have access to that much power."

"There's an investigation to figure out who else was involved. At this point, they suspect the school treasurer as well as someone at the bank." Millie had been texting Reid updates.

Mom pressed her hands against the counter. "How much did he take?"

Reid slid a cutting board across the counter to her, along with a couple of green bell peppers. He knew she processed things best when she was working. Sure enough, she began to dice the peppers into small pieces before sliding them into a bowl.

"I think they are still trying to get an exact number, but all the extracurricular clubs were hit the hardest. Drama, band, dance, and orchestra were completely wiped out. The biggest fund was the student activities budget. The homecoming dance is gone for sure, as well as all the normal back to school activities like the pancake brunch and the fun run."

The rhythmic sound of the knife hitting the cutting board was soothing to Reid. His mom looked up at him. "I know we have some extra funds tucked away. Do you think they would help?"

Reid shook his head. They could help with part of an activity, but that wouldn't be enough to restore what was lost. That would take many more hands.

As Reid talked with his mom, an idea formed. They were just one of the three big ranching families in the community. If he joined forces with the Stringham and Landon families, they should have enough connections between them to pull a fundraiser together for the kids.

Reid picked up his phone to text Millie and ask her about the idea, but then he lowered it. He didn't want to get her hopes up only to have them dashed if someone in the administration said no.

He kissed his mom on the cheek and headed out to his car. If there was any chance of his plan working, he needed help from the other residents of Old Ranch Road.

* * *

THE FOLLOWING WEEK, Reid offered to drive Bree to school.

"Why are you taking me? Is it so you can surprise Miss Millie?" Bree asked.

Reid shook his head. "Not exactly." Then he thought about why he was there. Millie had asked him for a magic wand, and that was what he was hoping to provide. He handed Bree a note. "Can you hold on to this for me? I'll text you when I want you to give it to Millie."

Bree's face lit up. "Does this mean you're going to start dating her again?"

"We'll see." He waited for Bree to enter through the double doors at the front of the school. Then he drove around the back and squeezed his Mustang between two large trucks. He figured Millie was already at school, but he didn't want to get caught if she was running late.

Fifteen minutes later, it was time. Reid walked to the front of the school where he met his cousin, Aaron Stringham and their neighbor, Mr. Landon.

He clapped each of them on the back. "Thanks for helping me with this, guys."

Mr. Landon nodded. "This school put up with my rowdy boys for years. I'm happy to give something back."

"I agree." Aaron straightened his hat. "I figure if a flood

tore through here, destroying the foundation of the school, the community would show up in droves to help. I don't think they'll bat an eye at helping to repair the damage from one corrupt principal."

"That's what I hope, too." Reid led the way to the principal's office where Mrs. Talmadge was waiting.

Forty-five minutes later, the trio of cowboys walked out of the school, their heads held high. Not only had they gotten approval to move forward with the pancake fundraiser and the homecoming dance, but they had a list of all the other ways they could help mitigate the damage Mr. Albertson had caused.

Reid leaned back in his Mustang and let the victory wash over him. He was rallying the troops for the school and for his sister Bree, but really, he was doing everything for Millie. It was the first on a long list of ways he hoped to win her back.

He pulled out his phone and sent a quick text to Bree. **It's time. Please give Millie the note whenever you see her.**

The three dots danced on his screen for a long time before Bree answered. **Done. Also, she looks cute today.**

Reid kept grinning the entire drive home. He couldn't wait for Millie's reply.

CHAPTER 22

Millie looked at the sea of faces in front of her. She recognized a few of the students as siblings from older classmates she had taught. Bree was sitting in the front row with a gigantic smile on her face. She kept peeking into her bag, but then she'd straighten up, giving Millie her full attention.

Halfway through class, Bree had raised her hand and asked to use the bathroom. She followed Millie to her desk in the back. When Millie gave her the hall pass, Bree slid a note across her desk with a wink. "Let me know if you need me to send anything back," she said.

Millie's heart leaped to her throat. There was only one person who passed notes to her, and that was Reid. The last time they had been passing notes, Millie found herself falling hard for the cowboy. She knew she should wait until the end of class to read what he had written, but she was too impatient for that. It was time to give the students an activity to work on so she had a free moment.

"Class, I want you to get in groups of four and brainstorm a list for me. I need a pair of characters, a problem they have to solve, and the obstacle that is standing in their way. We're going to be sharing them with the class and voting for a favorite, so make them good."

There was a loud shuffling of chairs before the room filled with the low clamor of students working. Millie opened Reid's note, flattening it out on the desk in front of her.

Millie,

Will you go to the pancake breakfast with me?

The words didn't make sense. She had spent a lot of time over the past couple of days telling Reid how frustrated she was that the first event of the year couldn't happen. Obviously, she couldn't go with him.

She skimmed past the check yes or no boxes, getting to the fine print at the bottom. *Call me when you get a break. I have a lot to tell you.*

The butterflies in Millie's stomach picked up their dance. Even though classes were only an hour long, Millie felt like the clock had stopped. She tried to focus on each group of students as they presented their ideas to the class. Instead, her mind kept wandering back to Reid's note. Why would he ask her a question he knew she wouldn't be able to accept?

The minute hand crawled by. She pulled Bree to the side when the bell rang. "Can you come back in the afternoon to pick up my answer for Reid?"

Bree's happy smile said it all. "For sure. I'll see you after school."

"Thanks, Bree." Millie waited until the door closed before she pulled out her phone. She had her prep period next, which would give her plenty of time to check in with Reid before she got back to work.

"Did you get my note?" Reid asked. He sounded entirely too cheerful when he answered the phone.

"I did, but I don't understand it. Reid, you know we had to cancel the pancake breakfast."

Reid gave a low chuckle that immediately lifted her spirits. "About that. Some of us didn't think it was a good idea for the kids to have to pay for Mr. Albertson's dishonesty. We spoke to Mrs. Talmadge, and she approved our plan."

Millie pressed a hand to her chest. "I'm not following. What plan did you present to the principal?"

"We're welcoming those kids back to school with the traditional pancake breakfast."

Reid's words hung in the air. They didn't make any sense, and yet there was hope that blossomed in Millie's heart.

"How can you do that? You've already been generous enough with the school." Millie's hands were trembling. She ran her hand up and down the bracelet she wore, trying to understand.

"I talked with a few of the people in the community. We agreed that we're going to make things as normal for these kids as we can this year. I know that you and the parents will eventually get the school back on its feet. In the meantime, there's a group of us who want to ease that transition."

"So, you're having the breakfast?" Millie didn't know what to say.

"Yes. We're having the pancake breakfast. But we're going to make it the biggest fundraiser this school has ever seen. The proceeds from that will start the seed money that will continue to grow through the year."

Millie could tell Reid was excited, but she had been on the parent/teacher committees before. Getting donations to run the events was difficult. Reid couldn't possibly understand what he was trying to do.

"Do you know how much we rely on donations from the community?" Millie didn't want Reid's hopes to be dashed. "Most of the businesses already donated earlier in the year."

Reid chuckled again. "How about you worry about your class, and let me and my guys handle the rest? We've got a plan. If you want to come over tonight, I'd love to show you everything we've put in place. Or you could meet me at the event and be surprised."

Millie tilted back in her office chair, so she was staring at the ceiling. "I could tell you my answer, but then poor Bree wouldn't have anything to hand back to you."

"I can't wait until she's home. I'll be waiting to hear what your answer is going to be."

Millie hung up the phone and turned her attention to the paper in front of her. She marked the yes box with a heart. To the side she wrote a short note. *Thanks for saving the day, cowboy. My answer will always be yes.*

By the time the day ended, rumors were flying around school about the three families from Old Ranch Road stepping up to take care of the school. As promised, Bree showed up to grab the note for Reid.

"Did you know about Reid's plans?" Millie asked.

Bree shook her head. "I'm still not sure what they are, but if we get our school back, I'm happy."

That was the reminder Millie needed. If the students were happy, so was she.

* * *

TWO WEEKS LATER, Millie pulled up to the park. Every spot in the parking lot was filled, with cars and trucks lining the sides of the street. She pulled into a spot labeled Teacher Parking and climbed out.

Reid was standing behind a griddle, shoulder to shoulder with the men and women from the three biggest ranching families in the town. They were an impressive sight, with their cowboy hats casting their faces in shadow. Millie recognized Porter, Thomas, Reid, Hope, and Mom Matthews, along with several faces she didn't know.

As Millie got closer, she giggled. Each of the cowboys was wearing an apron, no doubt provided by the parents of the students. Some of the aprons had more flowers on them than a garden. There was a sizzle of the sausage and bacon being turned on the griddle.

Millie waited her turn in line, her mouth watering at the smell of bacon. The pancake breakfast was a tradition that had been started by the first senior class of the school. They wanted to support the drama kids in a Shakespeare competition, so they pulled the resources together and bought a few bags of pancake mix. Everyone was surprised when the community showed up and paid $5 per plate for sub-par food. Over the years, the food improved but the smiles on the student's faces never changed. They looked forward to giving back.

This year's line moved much slower than the lines from the past. Millie guessed it was because the chefs were mostly cowboys who were more comfortable in the fields than in the kitchen. As she got closer, she changed her mind. Each person had a sign and a jar in front of them.

For extra donations, you could upgrade your plate. The men had a variety of options to choose from, from specialized animal pancakes to spatula tricks while they flipped the meat. The family in line in front of Millie asked what would happen if they donated an extra $100.

Porter gave a loud whistle, and the helpers dropped their utensils. They launched into a short song, swaying their hips while they sang at the top of their lungs. After the song, they removed their hats and took a bow, before jumping back to their stations.

Everyone in the park cheered, from the families scattered at picnic tables to the people still waiting in line. Millie got the feeling that the cowboys had been performing more than a few times already.

Her cheeks hurt from smiling when she finally got to the front of the line. She pulled out a twenty-dollar bill and held it out to Porter, but he pushed it away. "I'm pretty sure you're going to want to put that in Reid's tip jar." He gave her a wink and turned his attention to the family waiting behind Millie.

Millie's butterflies were doing aerials in her stomach when she came to a stop in front of Reid's station. There was a sign, in bold letters, that said "Surprises, $5 each." Millie looked at Reid, in a giant pink ruffled apron, and her heart skipped a beat.

"I'd like a surprise, please." She slipped her $20 into the jar, which was close to overflowing.

"She said she wants a surprise, fellas." Reid nudged the men on either side of him.

The volunteers stepped back from their food stations. They huddled together, with Mom Matthews giving each person a pat on the back. The helpers elbowed each other as they formed a line.

"Music," Thomas hollered.

A country song began to play over the loudspeakers. Reid reached under the table and pulled out a bouquet of flowers. He handed it to Millie before he backed up, careful not to break eye contact.

There was a roar from the audience behind the cowboys when they began their line dance. Millie giggled watching them while they swayed back and forth. The men jumped as one, turning to face the parking lot, all except for the cowboy on the end who was turned the wrong way. As he spun to face the right direction, Millie caught the glimpse of something white taped to his back.

Tears pricked at the corner of her eyes when the men turned again, their backs to her. Across each cowboy's shirt was taped a piece of paper. A few of the men were out of order, but it didn't matter. Reid's message was easy to read.

Teacher, will you go ? dance to the homecoming with me

One of the students ran up and arranged the cowboys in the right way. *Teacher, will you go to the homecoming dance with me?* The words were in order now, but Millie was already running towards Reid.

She jumped into his arms, letting him swing her in a circle. "Yes," she whispered. Then she turned to the crowd and cupped her hands to her mouth. "I said yes."

Reid's response was drowned out by the cheers and whistles.

This time there was no hesitation when he lowered her to the ground. He pulled her close for a soft kiss, and then held her hand high in the air.

"Reid," Thomas called. "You're going to burn the pancakes."

"Sorry," Reid called. He tipped his hat to Millie. "Enjoy your breakfast, Ma'am."

Millie took her plate and went to sit at a table with her friend Sheila. "I don't know how they pulled this off."

Sheila nodded. "They've been a hoot to watch. I don't know how we're going to go back to our regular pancake breakfast after this."

Millie's heart was full watching the line that never seemed to end. She couldn't see how much money they were making, but the constant antics from the cowboys and cowgirls made her think that it was going to be a lot.

She rested her chin on her hands and watched her favorite cowboy of all. The school year was a time for new beginnings, and this was a story she was eager to write.

* * *

A FEW NIGHTS LATER, Millie peered out the window. She was getting picked up for a date, but this time, the only nerves she felt were flutters of excitement. After texting Reid every day, it was going to feel great to see him in person.

The pancake breakfast had been a resounding success, but Millie really hadn't had time to talk to Reid. Their relationship seemed to be back on, but Millie needed more than a cute homecoming invitation to go on. It was time to see where the relationship was heading for real.

Reid walked up to the door, a glint of gold at his waist. Millie's hand flew to her mouth while she doubled over laughing. She flung the door open. "I know this isn't our first date, so why are you wearing the belt buckle?" The buckle was just as garish as Millie remembered it to be.

Reid patted the belt. "It's a new start for me. Our first date was a disaster."

Millie had to agree. Getting a glass of water spilled down her lap by a jealous woman wasn't high on her list of favorite dates. "Yeah, it was pretty much a mess."

Reid nodded. "The second date wasn't much better. I had fun, but all we did was establish rules for fake dating. That's not the relationship I'm interested in now."

"I see." Millie bit the side of her cheek. "So, what are you hoping will happen this time around?"

Reid held his arm out. "I'm hoping that you'll come to dinner with me, and we'll be able to make some plans for the future. I know how it feels when we're dating, and I know how my life looks without you in it. I personally would like to move forward with you by my side."

There were a lot of emotions going through Millie's mind when she rested her hand in the crook of Reid's arm. "I'd like to explore that option, as well. I think we make a pretty good team."

The air blew gently across Millie's skin when she walked down the steps. It raised goosebumps on her arm. She knew that this time around, she wasn't going to let Reid go without a fight.

They were almost to the car when Millie stopped and held her hand out. "I'd like the belt buckle, please."

Reid's eyes were difficult to read when he unbuckled the belt and handed it over. "I haven't had anyone take it away before. I'm not sure what this means."

Millie walked back to her porch and set it on a step. "It means that I accept you for who you are. It means that you don't need to worry about pressure from your brothers or expectations from anyone other than yourself to be who you want to be. And it means that I plan to be the only woman in your life for the foreseeable future. You aren't going to be needing that belt buckle again."

Reid held his arms open wide and Millie walked into them. Her entire body relaxed when she rested her cheek against his chest. This was the place where Millie belonged. She closed her eyes when Reid wrapped her in a hug, holding her tight.

"My brothers are going to give me a hard time for this," Reid said.

"I know." Millie tilted her head up so she could study

Reid's face. "If they have a problem, they can take it up with me."

Reid's eyes were smoldering when he tilted his head. Millie met him halfway, sealing her words with a kiss.

When they separated, Millie's toes were quivering but her conviction was strong. She planned to kiss Reid in this same spot, over and over again, through all the seasons. If she was lucky, maybe Hazel's wedding bouquet was right, and a wedding would be in her future.

Reid rubbed his hand down Millie's back. "Sorry. I don't know where my manners are." He gave her an exaggerated wink. "I never kiss women on first dates, and I definitely don't kiss them before the date has even started."

Millie reached for his hand. "Funny thing. I'm the same way."

"Looks like we're already going to be in trouble." Reid held the car door open for Millie, pulling her close as he pressed his lips to her forehead. "I figure I may as well get used to this."

Millie's heart was floating when Reid settled into his seat. She leaned across the center console, giving him a quick kiss on his cheek. "Where are we headed?"

Reid tucked a strand of hair behind Millie's ear. "Wherever you'd like."

Millie leaned back against the cool leather of the seat and closed her eyes. "Surprise me, cowboy."

His response warmed her heart. "You've got it, teacher."

EPILOGUE - FOUR MONTHS LATER

Reid stood outside Millie's house, holding up a strand of lights with one hand while he swatted at the snowflakes that were falling with his other hand. "Remind me why we are hanging lights today? In this weather?"

Millie's face popped out from behind one of the pillars. "I told you. I only have two weeks for my Christmas break. I'm the last house on the street to decorate."

Her cheeks were bright red from the cold, but Reid recognized the determination in her eyes. If it was important to her, the house would be decked out just in time for Christmas.

He had offered to climb up a ladder and hang the lights from the roof, but Millie said she had a system worked out. Instead, he followed her, untangling the strands as he waited while she hopped up and down a step stool. When they reached the end of the lights, Millie held up the plug.

"Go stand on the sidewalk and close your eyes," she said. Reid laughed as he followed her directions. He turned to face the house, taking in the sight of Millie. She took his breath away every day.

"I said eyes closed," she reminded him.

Reid let his eyes drift shut, not daring to open them until he felt Millie by his side. She squeezed his hand, her gloves cool against his skin. Snowflakes bit against his cheeks but he kept his eyes shut.

"You can open them."

Reid glanced down at the woman in front of him, who was so excited about the Christmas season. Then he looked at the house.

Colorful lights surrounded each pillar, immediately brightening up the night. There were four pillars on the porch, and each one had been wrapped with red and white lights to look like candy canes.

Reid wrapped Millie in a hug, nuzzling her neck before he kissed her cheek. "They are perfect." He scooped her up in his arms and carried her towards the house while her laughter filled the air. "Can we go inside to warm up now?"

Millie was still laughing when he set her down on the porch. "We're not quite done." There was a red bin sitting near the front door that Reid had forgotten about.

He took the lid off the bin and pulled out a snowman with a lopsided smile. "I can't believe you kept these. I totally thought you'd repaint the faces."

"Why?" Millie held her hand out for the snowman. "I think it gives them character."

She placed the tallest snowman to the right of the door and held her hand out for the other two. They stood as a pair on the other side of the door. "What do you think?"

Reid crossed his arms and leaned back. "I think they are missing something." He pulled the blue scarf off his neck and looped it around the tallest snowman's neck. Then he set his cap on its head. "Much better."

Even though Reid would have chilly ears on his drive home, he liked the idea of part of him standing guard on Millie's porch.

"That's perfect." Millie opened her door and pulled Reid inside. "Now we can warm up."

Ten minutes later they were cuddled up under a blanket on the couch, blowing on cups of very hot cocoa. Reid slid his mug to the table and wrapped his arm around Millie.

Over the past four months, he had gotten to see a lot of sides of Millie. He had seen her when she was worried about the students in her class, unsure if she was going to be able to help them enough. He had cheered with her when she got the golden apple award for her work the first semester of school. He had laughed with her when they chaperoned student activities, jumping into the games like they were students themselves.

The homecoming dance had happened, and thanks to the overwhelming support of the community, so had the winter formal. Because the funds were restored, the kids were able to go to their competitions, and so far, they were placing in the top three with everything they did.

Millie told Reid it was because he and the ranchers had stepped up, but Reid knew the truth. The students were thriving because they had teachers like Millie who believed in them. It made him happy that his little sister was getting to experience that support. Instead of a heartbreaking year,

Bree got to be a regular student who only had to worry about the teenage drama that was normal for kids her age.

Reid pressed a kiss to the top of Millie's head.

"What was that for?" Millie asked. "Not that I'm complaining." She put her cocoa mug down and turned to face him.

There were a lot of thoughts running through Reid's head. "Have I told you how incredible you are?"

Millie snuggled into his side. "Let's see. I think you may have once or twice today."

Reid rubbed her shoulder. "I don't understand how or why you chose me, but I'm so glad you did. I'm the guy who messed everything up, and now I'm the guy who gets to date you."

Rex chose that moment to come jump on the couch between them. Millie laughed, wrapping her arms around her dog's neck. She cupped her hands over Rex's ears. "Don't tell Rex, but you're the most important man in my life. I'm so grateful that we were paired up for Thomas and Hazel's wedding. You've changed me for the better."

Reid ran a hand through his hair. "I don't know. You might just be keeping me around because I'm good at decorating. Speaking of which, what's next on our list?"

Millie groaned and leaned her head back. "Is it bad to say that I just don't want to have any more holiday cheer today? We still have the tree to put up and I was going to make a garland for the coffee table, but I'm exhausted."

Reid scratched beneath Rex's chin, smiling when the dog licked his hand. "I have an idea. What if we finish the rest tomorrow?"

The couch shifted when Millie turned around to point at an empty space in the family room. "It looks so bare without a tree."

"It looked that way yesterday and the world didn't end." Reid was teasing, but he had a goal in mind. He wanted to make sure Millie enjoyed every minute of her break.

She opened her mouth to protest but Reid stopped her with a kiss.

"I have a new plan. What if we stay on the couch and watch one of those cheesy Christmas movies you're always talking about? You're supposed to be on break, right?"

Millie nodded.

"So, let's take a break. I'll come by tomorrow and help set up the tree. In fact, I'm pretty sure Hope and Bree would love to come help decorate. They did a great job on the tree at home." Reid's house had been decked out since the day after Thanksgiving, but he didn't want Millie to feel bad that she was so far behind.

"I like that idea." Millie patted the couch and Rex hopped off her lap, curling up on the cushion beside her. She reached for the remote and pulled the blankets up to her chest. Then Millie bent her knees and tucked her legs to the side, leaning in so she was nestled in Reid's favorite spot right against his heart.

"You always know how to make me feel better," Millie said. "Thanks for being my rock."

Reid kissed the top of Millie's forehead. "I am the lucky one. I love you."

The smile that lit Millie's upturned face warmed Reid's heart more than any amount of cocoa ever could.

She tilted her face up and kissed him softly. "I love you, too."

Reid's heart was full when the movie began to play. He knew Millie wanted to date for a full year before considering marriage, but he was happy to take his time getting to know this amazing woman. He couldn't wait to see what adventures the next season brought. If all went well, by this time next Christmas, Millie would be wearing a very pretty diamond on her finger.

Spring, summer, fall or winter. No matter the season, Reid was ready to handle the hurdles of life with the teacher by his side.

Thanks for joining me on Reid and Millie's adventures. They will continue to make appearances through the Elk Mountain Series as their relationship grows. The family saga continues in A Secret Sunrise for the Cowgirl.